REBEL SPELL

SALEM SUPERNATURALS 1

LISA CARLISLE

LISACARLISLEBOOKS.COM

JOIN MY VIP READERS LIST!

Don't miss any new releases, giveaways, specials, or freebies! Access EXCLUSIVE bonus content.

Join the VIP list at *lisacarlislebooks.com* and download Darkness Rising, a shifter / vampire gothic story, part of the Chateau Seductions series, as well as other free reads and exclusive content!

Join my Facebook reader group!

For E.

Always.

COPYRIGHT

Rebel Spell

Edited by Natasha Larry

Cover design by Molly Burton of Cozy Cover Designs

Find out more about the author and upcoming books online at lisacarlislebooks.com, facebook.com/lisacarlisleauthor, or @lisacbooks.

Created with Vellum

ABOUT REBEL SPELL

By Lisa Carlisle

A hapless witch. A broken vampire.

And a mysterious death that brings them under the same roof.

When I, Nova Adams, learn I've inherited a house in Salem, I'm sure it's a mistake.

Besides, I have zero desire to return to a town where I'm an outcast.

The surprises continue when I meet my tenants, including a broody vampire and a foodie wolf shifter.

But I'm only staying around long enough to sell the house.

Even when they convince me to go to a Halloween ball.

Even when I agree to pretend to be the vampire's girlfriend.

Even when I discover his softer and oh-so-sexier side.

Because a witch without magic in Salem makes as much sense as a pig with wings. And I've never seen one fly.

CHAPTER 1

NOVA

The train jerked, and I lunged forward, knocking my paperback to the floor. *Wicked bats and flying monkeys,* I cursed in my head. The erratic jolt shook me like some seismic shifting. When I ricocheted back in my seat, I bumped into the twenty-something guy in full manspread mode beside me.

"Hey, take it easy," manspread guy said in a thick Brooklyn accent. He raised his hand as if to punctuate his point with a silent *whatsamattawidyou*?

"Sorry, the subway shaking knocked me off balance." I gave him a sheepish look before picking up my book, using as little as possible of two fingers, and then tried to shake off the quintillion subway germs that leaped onto it. I then reached for the hand sanitizer in my bag.

I glanced at the other passengers. No one else seemed to react. Odd. Then again, this was New York City, and trains lurched all the time. Still, I would think there would be some grumbling or outright swearing with the movement causing instability. It was sure to disturb others, maybe even cause chaos with coffee spills.

"What are you talking about, lady?" Brooklyn guy asked with disdain.

Good question. A few people nearby flashed a wary glance, castigating me as a weirdo before returning to the customary vacant train stare.

"Never mind," I replied.

Maybe where I was sitting gave me the most impact. Yet, manspread guy hadn't reacted, and neither had the woman on the other side of me whose incessant phone-scrolling hadn't ceased since she'd boarded the stop after me.

Strange tingles buzzed inside my body. What was causing them? They seemed to drift, falling like some sort of vibrant confetti. I placed a hand on my chest. The heat of an electric buzz intensified.

Within a red hot New York minute, a sheen of perspiration coated my skin. It was October. I shouldn't be sweating like this. Sure, I had my happy yellow peacoat on, but it wouldn't turn me feverish.

That mysterious sensation diminished and disappeared by the next stop. Crap, I probably stank. What a way to roll into work.

I pictured Mary Katherine Gallagher sniffing her pits on *Saturday Night Live* and told myself not to do anything so obvious. Instead, I bent my head to take an inconspicuous sniff. When I was hit by a whiff of subway and people on subway, I blocked my nostrils with my forearm. What did I expect considering where I was? Sweaty people and B.O. weren't a rarity.

Brooklyn dude stood and walked to the far end of the train, shooting me a look of disgust. What a peachy start to a Monday morning—gaining consternation from fellow passengers.

I put the incident aside as I climbed out of the subterranean world and lost myself among the columns of buildings stretching to the clouds. I'd been living here for a year and loved it, most of the time. The pulse of the city left me energized. The downside was the constant struggle to scrape up money for food, rent, and school loans each month. My low-level job as an editorial assistant didn't pay much, so I had a part-time waitressing job. It seemed all I did was work. So much for moving here to experience all that New York had to offer.

The rest of the day proceeded like the many before. I worked a double, first at the children's publishing house dealing with the grunt work of spreadsheets and slush piles, and then at the diner near Broadway. At least I had my dinner half-price that night. I thought it should have been free, but management didn't consult me on my preference.

It wasn't until a few days later that everything changed. I had a voice mail from a lawyer with the Salem Supernatural Network. Her name was Lorna LaRue. She asked me to call her back as soon as possible.

Salem.

I exhaled and stared off into the distance. I hadn't been there since I finished high school and had no desire to return. A witch without magical talent had as much value there as a prince in a castle cursed to live as a toad.

An incident when I was a kid flashed in my brain, when I'd almost burned the family house down. My throat clogged as if still filled with smoke.

Shuffling into the tiny galley kitchen, I filled a glass with ice water and gulped it as if it would douse the flames in my mind.

And what the heck was this Salem Supernatural Network? I groaned. The name pretty much spelled it out for me—it had to be a network for supernaturals in Salem.

The strange fluttering in my chest that originated when the train jolted me returned. What the what? It was like someone pressed a button to turn it back on.

I snorted. The one pressing the metaphorical button was me, and it had to only be nerves. I leaned forward, bracing myself with the edge of the counter for support, and tried deep breathing to rein in my anxiety or whatever it was that agitated me.

Suck it up, buttercup. With one more deep inhale, I tried to summon courage.

Carrying my water over to the living room, I sat on the tattered brown couch of unknown origin one of my roommates had brought home. After one more sip, I picked up the phone to call the lawyer, Lorna LaRue. What alliteration. *Lawyer Lorna LaRue. Lawyer Lorna LaRue.*

Focus.

When Lorna answered the phone, she relayed information that would knock the stripes off a tiger. "Your aunt, Margaret Goodwell, recently passed away. She left some of her estate to you, including her house in Salem."

I pulled the phone from my ear and stared at it like I'd detect something to indicate this was a prank. Raising the phone back to my ear, I said, "That can't be right. I barely knew her." The last time I'd seen her was when I was a kid.

"It was what she wished," Lorna replied.

While I listened, stunned, Lorna summarized what happened. My aunt had been found unresponsive in her house and had died of heart failure. "As a witch with an affinity for the earth, she'd arranged for her ashes to be returned to the earth on her passing. It has been done. In addition to the house, she left you some money to help with the upkeep. Can you come to Salem so we can take care of the paperwork in person?"

It took a few seconds for my brain to catch up to this minefield of surprises.

After mentally calculating how many vacation days I had, I figured I could go up on Monday so I wouldn't lose too many waitressing shifts. How many days would it take to deal with whatever went along with inheriting a house?

"One second, please. I need to pull out my planner." That was how I kept my life under control, spicing up my schedule and to do lists with fun stickers. I glanced at the days ahead. "How about Monday?"

"Terrific, I'd suggest spending a week or two in town, if you can."

"That long?" I groaned inside. I didn't have that sort of vacation time. Plus, I needed my waitressing income to pay my part of the rent. I'd use up all the vacation time I'd saved to return to a town I had zero desire to visit.

"These things take time," Lorna said. "You'll also inherit just over fifty thousand dollars."

Fifty thousand? Wow. That would cover many, many waitressing shifts.

"Depending on what you do with the house, we'll need to discuss the lease for the existing tenants," Lorna added.

"Tenants?" Why was I repeating her like a confused parrot?

Confused was among the many emotions running rampant in my brain, playing hopscotch with shock and wonder.

Oh my, this made me a landlord. I was used to paying one, not being one.

Yikes. Home ownership already stressed me out, and I hadn't even seen the house yet.

After we arranged a time to meet, Lorna ended the call. I put the phone in my jeans pocket, grabbed my coat, and climbed down the stairs to head out of my apartment. What I needed was to clear my head. The scents from the Chinese restaurant at floor level filled the air. Why would my aunt leave the house to me? Didn't she have anyone closer? Why hadn't my mother told me that she'd died? They weren't close, but still.

The only person who could answer these questions was my mom. She was in Myrtle Beach with some rich guy who loved to golf.

I meandered over to a park and kicked through the fallen leaves on the concrete path. The trees had morphed to their autumn splendor, a dress change to reds, oranges, and yellows before the leaves took their dramatic plunge to the earth. The October evening was brisk enough to keep the visitors sparse, and I found an empty bench without a problem.

I Facetimed my Mom. When she answered, her dark blond hair was in rollers. "Oh, hi honey. I'm getting ready to go out with the Donnellys tonight. You remember me telling you about them? They moved here from Connecticut to retire early. He made a killing in the stock market."

My mom could go on rambling through a conversation. If I didn't interject, we'd never get to the reason why I called. "Mom, I heard about Aunt Margaret."

"Oh." Her careful facade fell to a frown.

"You know she died, right?"

She avoided eye contact, staring at something at floor level. "I do."

"Why didn't you tell me?"

She brushed the hair from her temple behind her ear. "Well, you didn't really know her. I didn't think I had to tell you right away."

"She's your sister. We're blood."

My mom snorted and briefly met my gaze. "Just because you're related doesn't mean you'd be friends. Half of the time people who share blood would avoid each other at a party at all costs." Her nostrils flared. "Even worse, you're expected to donate kidneys or some other vital organ."

I was an only child and often fantasized about siblings. What would it be like to have a big brother who looked out for me or a little sister who annoyed me?

"Mom, this is your sister you're talking about. Your *only* sibling."

A flicker of pain flashed in her eyes, but then she pursed her lips in a bitter expression. "We haven't spoken in years and for good reason."

"What reason? You never told me."

She turned her head in dismissal. "A difference of opinion. It's no longer important."

"It seems to be with the way you've shut her out all these years."

My mother's lips parted, and she met my gaze again. "Can we talk about this at another time? I have to get ready."

Apparently, dinner with the Donnellys meant more to her than her sister. "Sure. I wanted to tell you what happened. I just got off the phone with her lawyer. Aunt Margaret left her house to me."

"What?" Her mouth opened wide. "Why would she do that?"

I tipped my head lower. "That's why I'm calling you."

"I mean, she barely knew you."

I exhaled. "I'm aware of this."

"Why would she leave you her house?"

Ah, another one of my mom's quirks. She'd answer my questions with her own. "I called to ask you that," I repeated.

Her brows drew closer. "Well, I don't know."

I clucked my tongue. If my mother didn't know, would anyone? "Didn't she have other family or friends who she'd think of before me?"

"She had friends, all right," my mother replied in a sardonic tone and wagged a finger. "Not the kind of people you'd want to associate with."

My mother's judgment about who was or wasn't suitable company could be questionable since she had issues with just about every friend I'd ever had. "What does that mean?"

She blinked twice. "Naturally, you'll sell that dump."

Ah, now she was avoiding my question, another Mom thing.

Was Aunt Margaret's house a dump? I kicked at some colorful fallen leaves at my feet. "I don't know. Not only haven't I processed this info yet, I haven't even seen the place. I'm going on Monday."

She scowled. "You're going to Salem?"

"Yes, I need to meet with the lawyer. There's paperwork. There are tenants."

Her lips tightened into a grim line as if the idea of it was distasteful. "Oh, the horror. My sister was a misfit magnet. She'd give a meal and a bed to any wayward witch or supernatural. You're better off getting rid of this headache as soon as possible." She gestured with a dismissive wave. "Deal with what you need to do and get out of there, and fast." She fixed a steady gaze on me. "Salem isn't good for you."

My pulse quickened. That had been my plan, but why was my mom acting so weird? We used to live there. "Why?"

"Trust me." She glanced off into the distance. "I really need to go."

I ended the unhelpful call and stared across the park.

Was there anyone I could see while visiting Salem? My close friend, Gianna, still lived there. We hadn't talked as often since we graduated from high school, but still stayed in touch. Weeks or even months could go by, and we'd pick up as if no time had passed. Since we were both considered outcasts, even in a town that celebrated its oddities, our bond stuck.

I texted her. *I'm coming in this weekend.*

Nice! You better come and see me and check out the club! Do you want to stay at my place?

Hmm, good question. I technically owned a house now and could probably stay there. Without knowing the situation or talking to the tenants first, that seemed a bit weird.

If you don't mind.

It would be great to catch up with Gianna. She was my closest friend growing up. As a half-siren, she had plenty of male attention, but the girls considered her a misfit like me. Although she'd left Salem to travel for a while, she returned and opened a retro rock club a few years ago on the North Shore, closer to Boston.

Of course not! It's been too long. Can't wait to see you so we can catch up in person.

There was plenty of that to do, especially because of the last few hours, and I didn't know what to make of it.

Over a stiff drink. Or three.

I know just the place, Gianna replied with a winking emoji.

DIEGO

After a long night on my feet working at the healing center, I trudged the final steps home before dawn. Well, what was home for now. After Margaret's death, my two roommates and I weren't sure what was going to happen. We'd rented the main part of the house from her while she lived in her private apartment. A witch, shifters, and vampire sharing a house was a freak fest even for this town, which was more accepting to supernaturals than most.

Her unexpected death was a tough blow, especially since I was the one who found her. We had separate apartments and shared a kitchen, but after none of us had seen her for a few days, I went to check on her. The look of shock on her face as she lay on her back, staring up at nothing, was now seared into my memory.

As a fairly new vampire, I should get used to losing friends who weren't cursed with immortality. This loss was another reminder that I shouldn't get too close to anyone. They'd all disappear one day.

Near the front door, the black mailbox with our house number perched out front appeared full. I grabbed the stash of envelopes since my roommates acted like they had an allergic reaction to mail and rarely brought it in.

Once I entered, the scent of frying eggs, bacon, and tomato sauce wafted over from the kitchen. Sebastian, my wolf shifter roommate, listened to the morning news as he cooked. It would reach fifty degrees on a sunny October day, not that I'd have the opportunity to experience that. He had his intense, I'm cooking, serious expression on his unshaven face. The apron he wore had a finger pointing at him with steam around it and read "Sizzling."

He glanced up. "Hey man, what's up?"

"I'm ready to sit on the couch and watch mindless reruns until I'm catatonic." I sat on the worn gray suede sofa in the living room area, dropped the mail on the cushion beside me, and turned to a comedy station on the TV. Since this was an open-floor space, I could see him zipping about.

"Rough shift, huh?" Sebastian asked. "I made plenty of food." He winked. "I'll add some extra blood to your eggs."

"Thanks, Seb. Just a little, though." I specified with my thumb and forefinger. Many vampires couldn't tolerate food, but for some reason, I could eat small portions. Too bad that ability didn't extend to being able to survive without blood.

"Okay, a small plate."

"Sebastian," I warned. "I know how you get. You're always trying to feed me pasta like an Italian grandmother."

"Okay, okay, one tiny scoop." He nodded at the pile beside me. "Anything for me?"

I picked up the mail and began to sort it. One envelope stood out. It was cream and the return address was printed in an ornate font from the Salem Supernatural Network. They helped supes like us live and navigate the human world, with things like finding jobs and apartments. I straightened and stared at the return address as if the letters could strike like a cobra.

"Here's something for all of us." After hesitating, I opened the envelope and read an invitation. My bottom lip twitched.

"What is it?" Sebastian asked.

"It's an invitation for a Halloween ball, hosted by the Salem Supernatural Network next weekend."

"Nice." Sebastian raised his hand into a fist. "If anyone knows how to throw a ball on Halloween, it's supes in Salem."

"Yeah, maybe." When I spotted the next envelope that was addressed to me, I opened it. Although my heart no longer beat the way it once did, I swear it jolted against my rib cage. It was her writing—the Ex Who Must Not be Named.

"Never mind," I said. "No way am I going now."

"Why not?"

I raised my brows. "*She's* going." I read the note to him.

. . .

Hi Diego,

I'll be in Salem next weekend. Going to the ball on Halloween. Hope we can catch up.

Diana.

Sebastian scoffed. "Diana will be there. Big deal. You can't hide from her forever."

"I can," I countered as I shifted on the couch. "And I think I will."

He opened the oven and glanced inside. After he closed it, he said, "Come on, Diego. You've been brooding in this house long enough. Your ex broke your heart. So what? You're not the first guy it's happened to, and you won't be the last."

"Yet, most guys don't have the side effect of immortality to go with their broken heart." Diana had convinced me to become a vampire two years ago so we could be together forever. Forever turned out to be six months.

"The ball is a perfect start for you to finally begin to live your undead life." Sebastian said.

Lucas entered the house wearing a pair of leather pants so tight, it brought my attention to his junk. Not what I wanted to see. His loose-fitting white shirt would suit a pirate.

"Mmm, mmm, mmm. I love living with a chef," Lucas said. "Smells good in here."

With a proud grin, Sebastian declared, "I'm making batches of my grandfather's special sauce."

"Eww, that sounds nasty," Lucas teased.

Sebastian moaned. "Everything with you is about sex."

Lucas shrugged and tipped his head. "What can I say? I was born this way."

"Says the poet who doesn't know it," Sebastian added.

I grumbled, "I need new roommates."

That was the last thing I wanted. These guys turned things around for me when I moved in. Both were born supernaturals in a human world, and they helped me navigate it better. They were my family now.

Lucas laughed. "I hope you have enough for me because I'm starving." He peeked into the pot Sebastian was stirring.

"You know it," Sebastian replied. "I make enough to feed an army." He gestured at Lucas. "Diego, you should be more like him."

"Hungry?" I quipped with arched brows.

Lucas grinned. "Dragons have voracious appetites."

"That's not what I mean," Sebastian scoffed. "Lucas knows how to live life."

"That's because he has one," I pointed out.

"I strive to enjoy every day," Lucas said with a cocky grin.

They didn't get it. "We're different. You don't have the concerns I have to deal with, like an aversion to sunlight." Aversion. More like death by sunlight. "Or a thirst for blood," I added. When I'd agreed to shuffle off the mortal coil to be with my ex, I'd romanticized our pairing too much and neglected to pay attention to the downside of being a living corpse.

"Yeah, well, I have a thirst for something else." Lucas plopped down next to me. "But it's entirely pleasant."

I groaned. "I don't want to hear about your latest exploits."

"Anything good?" Lucas flipped through mail addressed to him.

Sebastian said, "We got an invitation to a ball."

I handed Lucas the invitation.

He read it. "Cool."

"Guess who's being a poopy pants saying he won't go."

"What are you, five?" I asked Sebastian.

Lucas stared at me like I'd turned into a merman. "Are you insane? Think of all the hot witches who'll be there."

I gritted my teeth. "Don't care."

"Diana will be there," Sebastian explained.

"Screw that bitch," Lucas barked. "Pardon my French." He covered his mouth with mock demureness. "Forget that lecherous creature of the night."

"I'm not talking about this again." I crossed my arms. Why wouldn't they leave me alone? If I lived my life as a hermit, I wouldn't risk getting hurt again.

After I found a *Scrubs* rerun, I continued to flip through the mail, separating it into piles for the three of us. The last one was a letter addressed to current residents. I opened it, read the letter, and cursed.

"What is it now?" Sebastian stirred the sauce again. "Did we get invited to a carnal carnival that you're going to shoot down next?"

“Ha, ha, and no. It’s about the house.”

Sebastian put the spoon down and covered the pot. “What about it?”

“The new owner is going to come by on Thursday. It’s Margaret’s niece. Her name is Nova Adams.” I scowled.

“What’s the problem?” Sebastian asked. “You knew someone would inherit the house.”

“Exactly.” I nodded. “And we already talked about what may happen. She’ll probably raise the rent or sell it. Or, she might want to move in here and kick our sorry asses to the curb. Either way, we’re screwed and will have to find a new place to live.”

“You don’t know that,” Lucas dismissed.

“Want to bet?”

“Of course.” Lucas could never turn down the chance to gamble. “Twenty bucks you’re wrong.”

I shook his hand. “I hope I am. You know how much I hate change.” I flipped through the rest of the mail. “Bills. Bills.” I threw down the pile. “Ugh, I hate mail.”

Lucas rolled his eyes at Sebastian. “Vamps are so melodramatic.”

“Lack of sunlight makes them sullen,” Sebastian agreed.

I snorted. “We’ll see what happens. At least I’m being a realist and covering my junk before a woman comes along to kick me between the legs.”

Lucas smacked his lips together. “You’re wrong, Diego. If this Nova is anything like Margaret, she’ll be cool.”

I stood. "Then why haven't we ever heard of her? Margaret never mentioned Nova's name."

Neither Sebastian nor Lucas had an answer.

"Call me a pessimist, but I can't see how anything good will happen once this Nova woman arrives. We'll likely be out on our asses before you can say *witch, please*."

CHAPTER 2

NOVA

After leaving the Salem Supernatural Network with not only a set of keys to my aunt's house, but an invitation to a ball on Halloween (no, thank you), I drove the burnt orange Mini Cooper I'd rented to the address in Salem. I'm sure I'd been there when I was little, but I couldn't remember it. My aunt had lived on a tree-lined road in a residential area. With it being October, the leaves were changing to marvelous shades of sunset overhead, and fallen leaves blanketed lawns.

At the end of the road, a lavender house sat on the back of the lot. It had a gabled roof and circular rooms in a tower section leading up to a turret. "Wow. I own this?"

After I closed my mouth, I pulled into a spot in the long driveway before a two-car garage that could use a fresh coat of paint. The October day was partly cloudy, but not yet cold enough for it to be uncomfortable outside.

I climbed out of the Mini and walked around the exterior to examine the house. It was spacious for sure, but dated, and could use some repairs. It had several bay windows, but the shades were drawn. Hmm. It was late afternoon. Wouldn't the tenants want some sunlight? A porch extended out from the back door with several pots of mums.

The house appeared to have good bones in my limited viewpoint, and plenty of space, much more than I could ever use. I scrunched my nose as I assessed the condition of the roof, but what did I know? At least it wasn't crumbling. A fresh paint of coat, some yard clean up, and some new landscaping would go a long way, especially if I ended up putting the house on the market.

I snapped a picture with my phone and sent it to Gianna.

Looks stellar, she texted back. *See you soon.*

I walked to the front door. It was painted black and had an ornate brass door knocker with a ring hanging from a gargoyle's mouth. I rang the bell. The tenants knew I was coming, yet I still felt like an intruder.

The sound of movement behind the door was followed seconds later with it opening.

A man with dark hair, groomed beard, and blue plaid shirt smiled. I pegged him to be in his late twenties. "Hi. You must be Nova."

"I am." I extended my hand.

"Sebastian." He stepped aside and motioned for me to enter. "Come on in." Once he closed the door, he took my coat and hung it on a coat rack in the entryway. "It's a shame what happened to your aunt. She was a good person."

"Thank you." I pushed my hair out of my face. "This whole thing has been quite a shock."

"It was unexpected," Sebastian agreed.

He led me into the living room, which had high ceilings and a brick fireplace. The hodgepodge of furniture sat on an aged maroon oriental rug that covered the hardwood floor. A brown suede couch and a worn black leather recliner faced a flat-screen TV.

"Come on, I'll show you around." He continued the tour of the main level. The dining room had wood paneling and a built-in china hutch. "Our bedrooms are up there." He pointed to the staircase.

A guy with dark blond hair, high cheekbones, and blue eyes bounded down the stairs. He wore loose fitting black pants and a white shirt with the top two buttons undone. "Hey, there. I'm Lucas." He took my hand and kissed it. "Enchante."

"Lucas, save it," Sebastian noted with irritation. "Your mojo won't work on her."

"Mojo?" I repeated.

"I'm a dragon shifter." Lucas winked. "Ladies are often drawn to us." He patted his chest. "Must be our fiery nature. But don't worry, I'm just saying hello."

My tenant was a dragon shifter? It was funny how open they were with me. Was it because of their relationship with my aunt? What a strange setup she had with these guys. Still, who was I to judge? If it worked, it worked. I forced myself not to react like some clueless person hearing about supernatural beings for the first time. I grew up in a town of witches. Gianna and I had known of other beings while we were in school. Their true nature was that guarded because humans could be unpredictable with that knowledge. Maybe supes were more open these days, or they sensed who they could trust.

Then again, they could probably use magic to wipe my memory clean if they deemed me a threat.

I hesitated before asking the next question. It had been so long since I'd been around non-humans that it felt strange to come straight out and ask. Since Lucas had willingly offered the info, I figured it was okay to ask. "Are you all supes?"

"Indeed," Sebastian replied. "I'm a wolf shifter. Our other roommate, Diego, is a vampire." He motioned his hands to the side and grinned. "The best tenants she's had, according to your aunt." He motioned for me to follow him into the kitchen. It had a vintage French country feel with yellow and blue decor.

"The house has this main kitchen, which we all share." He pointed to a door opposite from where they'd entered. "Margaret lived in those rooms over there. There's a small eating area overlooking the backyard on her side."

I stepped into my aunt's space. The circular room had a cozy feel with a sofa, built-in bookshelves, and afghans. "Is her bedroom upstairs?" I asked.

"Yes. She slept on the second floor, where there's also a bathroom." Sebastian pointed up. "And her workspace is on the third floor in the finished attic."

I nodded to give the sense that I followed what he was talking about, although I knew nothing.

"Do you want to go look around on your own?" Sebastian asked.

"I will in a bit." It still felt intrusive to poke around in a stranger's space, even if she was my blood relative.

Sebastian led me back into the living room where Lucas sat on the sofa with a gray cat beside him. He pet the long-haired furball. "This is Shadow, because he often follows me around like one. Hope you're okay with cats."

"Sure." I walked over and extended my hand. Shadow glanced at it from bright green eyes and sniffed me. I bent down and rubbed his cheek.

When I stood, a man wearing all black stared at me from near the fireplace.

I gasped. "Where did you come from?"

His glowering turned more intense. The reddish glint in the whites around his bright blue eyes gave him a feral look. I stepped backward and covered my chest with one hand. My heart pounded beneath my fingers.

Whoever he was, his glowering didn't bode well for me.

My breath came quicker as our gazes remained locked. Something about his stare intimidated, yet fascinated me.

Sebastian said, "Oh, that's Diego."

A thickness swelled in my throat. I swallowed. "Hi, there."

"Hello," Diego replied in a gruff tone. Then he scowled and headed upstairs.

I furrowed my brows. What the hell was that about?

"Don't mind Diego," Sebastian dismissed. "You know how vampires get."

"Not really."

Sebastian exhaled. "Maybe he's hangry." He shrugged one shoulder. "He might be more surly than usual today because he's worried about what you'll do with the place."

Ouch. I hadn't even been in the house for long before the elephant galloped into the room and skidded to a halt beside me.

"Yeah, well, that's something I'll need to consider," I admitted, not committing to anything.

"Of course," Sebastian said.

Lucas gestured to the sofa. "Have a seat."

After I did, I asked them, "How long have you lived here?"

"About a year-and-a-half," Sebastian replied. "We found your aunt through the Salem Supernatural Network and were lucky to do so. It's tough to find someone who will rent to supes."

I adjusted my position on the sofa. "Are you trying to make me feel guilty?"

Sebastian covered his chest. "No, of course not." His tone gave him away. He stood. "Where are my manners? What can I get you to drink? Tea? Lemonade?"

"Lemonade would be great."

They had to be worried about their living situation, and I didn't blame them. I distracted myself by petting Shadow.

"He loves chin rubs," Lucas said.

I gave it a shot and was rewarded with the sounds of a purring machine.

"He likes you." Lucas grinned with approval.

When Sebastian returned and handed me a glass of lemonade, I thanked him. "I understand why you'd be concerned about what

I'm going to do with the house, and I would be, too. But I don't yet know."

Sebastian exchanged a glance with Lucas before he leaned forward and addressed me. "I get it. This has been sprung on you. I apologize if we came off as pushy."

I nodded and then sipped the lemonade. It was cool and had the perfect combination of tartness and sugar and something I couldn't identify. "This is delicious by the way."

"Margaret taught us how to make it," Lucas said. "She added a bit of bergamot from the garden."

"Ah, that's what I couldn't place," I replied.

"Your aunt was amazing at whipping things up—recipes, potions, spells, any kind of concoction," Lucas said. "She had such a green thumb and taught me a lot about gardening. I bet you're just as talented."

I stared at the rug. "I'm afraid not."

"Surely you must share some of her skills," Sebastian prodded.

I shook my head and admitted, "No. Not only am I terrible at keeping any plants alive, I haven't even attempted to do magic in years."

"Why not?" Lucas scratched his chin as he peered at me in question.

I squeezed my lips together since I didn't know these guys well. They'd been pretty forthcoming thus far, so I admitted, "I was never any good at it." After taking another sip of my lemonade, I redirected back to them. "Tell me about yourselves."

Lucas leaned back on the sofa and announced with pride, "I'm a dancer."

Sebastian coughed and muttered, "Stripper."

"Exotic dancer." Lucas turned to Sebastian with a frown.

This appeared to be a common interchange between them. So Lucas was a dragon shifter and an exotic dancer. Picturing women throwing money at him and swooning made me smile. "What do you do, Sebastian?"

"I'm head chef at a restaurant nearby." He beamed. "What about you?"

"I work in children's publishing." I left out the low-level position and pay and the side job as a waitress. No need to admit how I'd gone to New York to make it big in the publishing world, yet after three years hadn't gotten far. I glanced upstairs to where the sulky vampire had disappeared. "What about Diego?"

"He works at a healing center downtown," Sebastian replied.

Although I had more questions about what exactly that entailed, I decided not to pry. After finishing my lemonade, I thanked them and stood. Time to explore my aunt's rooms. If I wanted to untangle this situation, I needed to figure out what thread to start with first.

DIEGO

I hadn't been able to keep from staring at Nova, my thoughts clouding with lust. Envisioning things I shouldn't do, I'd forced myself to keep control. I rarely drank from humans anymore since I hated the concept, but had to practically bury my feet through the floorboards to keep myself from walking over to her. Ultimately, I'd chosen to flee before doing something stupid I'd regret.

After I'd run from the room, I listened from the top of the stairs. Her scent had hit me like a sudden storm, sending electric vibrations through my body. It had a hint of rose water and a delicate aroma that ignited stark hunger. My fangs had pierced through my gums, itching to sink into that slim pale neck, which was partially exposed by a one-sided braid. I hadn't felt a yearning like that since I'd been newly turned, but it was different. It wasn't just a thirst for her blood, but a desire for *her*.

What the hell? She was a stranger.

A few minutes later, Sebastian came upstairs, where I still listened from the hallway outside our rooms.

"What's wrong with you, man?" he asked.

"What?" I asked with faux innocence, knowing full well he'd caught me eavesdropping.

"You just put the rude in brood."

I glanced away. "What are you talking about? I said hello to her."

"No, you lurked in the shadows like some creepy Nosferatu and scared the crap out of Nova."

He pretty much called it. I scowled. There was no excuse. With a shrug, I dismissed him. "I can't help it if she's skittish."

Sebastian narrowed his eyes. "You're keeping something from me."

"Okay, fine. It was her scent," I admitted, pacing through the hall. "I was overwhelmed by the urge to bite her."

Sebastian slapped his forehead. "You can't attack our new landlord."

I groaned. "Of course I won't."

He shook his head. "That's a way to ensure the eviction you're so worried about."

"I said I won't," I repeated.

Sebastian exhaled with a low whoosh. "What are you going to do now?"

I stared at him. "About what?"

"Nova."

What was he talking about? "Nothing."

"No, you need to talk to her and try to fix that horrible first impression. Drink a pouch of blood first so you don't go over there all feral."

I growled. "Fine." I threw one hand up. "I'll go be more chipper and kiss her ass like you and Lucas just did."

Sebastian turned his hand palm up. "We weren't kissing ass, we were being cordial," he said. "You should try it sometime. Maybe if you got out of the house more and met people, you'd get more practice."

"I meet plenty of people at work." That was an exaggeration. I mostly worked alone in the lab during the night shift and barely saw anyone. "I'll go handle it."

I walked over to her apartment and found the door open. About to announce my presence, the words petrified in my throat. Nova faced the windows with her hand on the string. She was about to open the sun-blocking shades.

"No!" The sun! My undead heart jolted against my rib cage.

I rushed forward and tackled her. As she fell to the ground, she shrieked.

CHAPTER 3

DIEGO

Nova stared up at me with wide-eyed surprise. I was just as stunned.

My body pinned hers down. Worse, I was aware of her soft parts touching me, reminding me how long it had been since I'd been with a woman. It didn't help subdue that rush of desire that had captured my thoughts. And her fragrance—it was right in my face now. Tackling her probably wasn't the best option. It took all my self-control not to bend closer to her throat and sink my fangs into that enticing column of flesh.

In the next heartbeat, she shouted, "Get off me," and tried to squirm out.

I attempted to climb up, but as she grasped me, she ended up pulling me back down. My hand landed on her breast.

"Ah!" I reacted with an unmanly high pitch and yanked my arm away.

Our joint attempts to escape this compromising situation tangled us more. When her hand accidentally brushed my semi-erect shaft, I moaned. The already mortifying situation turned exponentially worse.

When she extricated herself out of the farcical mess, she sat up, breathing hard. "Why did you just attack me?"

Aye, aye, aye. "Attack *you*? You almost killed me."

After I stood, she stared at me with confusion. "What?"

"I'm a vampire. The sunlight would fry me like an egg on a griddle." I walked over and offered her a hand and helped her get to her feet.

She narrowed her gaze and folded her arms around herself. "Why did you sneak up on me?"

Avoiding looking at her, I replied, "I was trying to come over here and be friendly after I realized how frosty I might have come off." *While fighting an urge to taste your blood.* I shrugged to feign nonchalance and mask the discomfort with how I'd botched that up with some epic flair. "So I came to welcome you properly."

She laughed with disbelief. "I wouldn't say there was anything proper about that greeting."

I groaned. "Survival instinct." When I pictured an alternative reaction that I could have taken—namely stepping back into my apartment and away from the sunny death ray—I cringed. After that unexpected reaction to her scent, I definitely wasn't on my best behavior.

"Sorry, I tackled you." I shuffled from one foot to the other. What could I say to fix this situation? Uh, pretty much nothing. "I'm-uh-going to go now."

Idiot, idiot, idiot, I cursed myself.

After I headed out, leaving her bewildering aroma behind, I almost ran into Sebastian. "What happened? I heard shouting."

I scowled at him. "Great advice, man."

"What did you do?" he asked with stern curiosity.

I'd tackled my new landlord to avoid an excruciating death. "Listened to you. And now I'm regretting it."

Sebastian knew nothing about being a vampire. I was better off brooding than burning.

NOVA

A vampire had tackled me because I'd almost torched him. That incident was a sour cherry on a melted sundae.

I replayed it in my head at least a dozen times before I drove over to Gianna's. She'd given me the key code to access her townhouse. After a long, long day, I was ready to relax, and plopped onto the sofa the second after I entered.

Still, I was too rattled to rest. The way that Diego had stared down at me with that dark hunger in his eyes woke up parts of me that had long been dormant. Although I'd been out of practice for some time, the stiffness against my thigh wasn't something I'd misidentify.

And a part of me liked it.

What a great start to my return to Salem—I almost murdered my tenant and then got turned on when he'd knocked me to the ground.

Maybe some relaxing music would help soothe me. I found a mellow mood playlist on my phone and then curled up with a book and some jasmine tea on her blue velvet sofa. I read a few chapters of a New England mystery while I sipped my tea. Gianna was working at her club, the Danger Zone, and told me to stop by for a drink later.

After eight, I changed into a pair of black jeans and a long-sleeved burgundy top and drove down Route 1 to her club. It was north of Boston, so I was able to avoid the city. Even better, it had free parking.

The black brick club with the small sign reading *Danger Zone* seemed low key, but once I stepped inside, that changed. The club had Gianna's signature all over it. Gianna loved vintage clothing, music, and styles, and this club reflected a retro rock feel. With the dark walls, skull and crossbones, and dungeon theme, it had the ambiance of an 80s Motley Crue video. The Scorpions' "Rock You Like a Hurricane" blared throughout the space.

That pretty much seemed to be the effect that Gianna had on the male clientele, many of whom were gaping at her. She stood near the beer taps, talking to a bartender with electric blue hair. Gianna's dark hair had bright red streaks in it that matched the blood red of her lipstick. She stood statuesque in spiky boots, and her slinky black dress clung to her impressive curves. Dressed hot enough to lure sailors to leap off their ship head-first into the sea. She'd have guys falling all over even if she didn't have siren blood.

Once she ended the conversation, she turned away and spotted me.

"Nova!" She walked over with her arms outstretched and embraced me. With her heels adding to her height, I stood like a doll next to her. Heels were not my friend. Any time I attempted to wear them, that decision was followed by more regret than drinking a scorpion bowl on an empty stomach. Since I favored the petite section of the women's clothing section, it didn't help my vertical challenge.

"How are you, Gianna?" I asked once we pulled apart.

"Splendid," she gestured around the club. "This place keeps me busy." She leaned closer and whispered in a conspiratorial tone, "And satiated."

I laughed. Gianna thrived on sexual energy, which she claimed was part of her siren blood. "It was pretty smart of you to lure your conquests to walk into the door."

"And pay for the pleasure." She gestured toward the bar and grinned.

I motioned to the decor. "I like the vintage vibe. It's totally you."

"There are a zillion clubs that are just clones of each other, know what I mean? I needed something different. And since 80s and 90s nights are so popular, I figured why not make it part of the theme?" She turned both hands up.

"True." I glanced around. The club had plenty of patrons and it was still early. Quiet Riot's "Cum on Feel the Noise" played next. I guessed that later on, this place might be packed and the cash registers full.

Gianna placed her hand on mine. "Sorry about your aunt."

"Thanks," I muttered, feeling odd to hear condolences about a woman I barely knew. "This whole situation is strange. I still don't get why she'd leave the house and everything in it to me."

She pulled her hand back and turned it palms up. "She wanted you to have the house for some reason. What did you think about it?"

I exhaled with a sigh that sounded more dramatic than I'd intended. "It's great. A beautiful old house with plenty of space. It's dated and has had add-ons over the years, and the layout is charmingly quirky." I bit my lip and tapped my fingers together. "But, there was something weird about her apartment."

"What?"

I tried to put my finger on it. "I don't know how to explain it. It was a strange atmosphere in her apartment that made me uncomfortable."

Sure, it could have been precipitated by the tension from being tackled by Diego, but I sensed it was more than that, especially when I'd entered my aunt's bedroom.

"Could be anxiety," Gianna offered.

"Possibly," I agreed.

"What do you think you'll do with the house?" She bent her head and smiled. "Any chance of you moving back here?"

"I don't think so." Tapping my fingers on the bar, I added, "I have a life in New York."

"A good one?" Gianna's gaze probed mine with an intensity that spoke a silent *Don't give me a bullshit answer.*

"I wouldn't say I'm on the top of the world." My shoulders tensed. It was more like struggling to keep from falling off a hamster wheel while juggling squirming snakes half the time. "But I have a job. Well, two."

"You can find a job—or two—here." She motioned through the club. "I'm sure I could get you some shifts here if you wanted."

"Thanks, but Salem and me?" My lips twitched. "A witch unskilled in magic is about as welcome here as—say, fur on a dragon."

Gianna laughed. "That's a bit of a stretch, but I get it."

"I also have an apartment there."

"You have a *house* here that you *own*. Even better."

"With tenants," I clarified.

"Have you met them yet?"

"Yes, I stopped by earlier. There are two shifters and a vampire living in the main part of the house. My aunt lived in a separate apartment, including tower rooms, which is pretty cool."

"How are they?" She arched her brows.

"Okay, I guess." Biting my lip, I then added, "Well, there was a bit of an embarrassing situation with the vampire, Diego."

Gianna's blue eyes sparkled. "Ooh, tell me. You know how I love stories with awkwardness."

That's because we'd collected a vast number between us growing up and often joked we should share them on stage at *Mortified*. But after puberty, Gianna had blossomed into a beautiful butterfly. Me? Well, at least I wasn't as gawky anymore.

I exhaled with a heavy sigh. "I almost fried him by sunlight when I started to open the shades. He tackled me to the ground. While we tried to get up, body parts of the opposite sex were accidentally grabbed."

Gianna covered her mouth and howled with laughter. "You felt up your tenant?"

I raised my chin as if I could crawl out of the depths of indignity. "It wasn't one sided. He grabbed my boob."

"This is the best. What a way to make an introduction!"

"Utterly embarrassing." Heat returned to my cheeks.

She raised her brows. "Is he cute?"

I pictured Diego with his dark hair and blue eyes, when they weren't masked by that reddish tinge. "I guess some people might consider him attractive."

"Are you *some* people?"

Averting eye contact, I shrugged. "Sure, he's okay."

Gianna clapped. "Even better. Does this mean it will lead to some hot monkey sex while you're in town?"

"Hell no," I protested. "After that incident, I'm hoping I can deal with what I have to do without seeing him again."

Gianna put her arm around my shoulder and steered me to the bar. "Come on, you need a drink."

After we sat at the bar and ordered cocktails, Gianna and I continued to catch up. I'd ordered a "Black Hole Sun," a variation on a Malibu Sunset. She'd selected a "Peaches," a Bellini-type drink she said was her current favorite.

"This is amazing." I took another sip. "It could be dangerous as it goes down so smooth." I'd have to stick to one, though, as I was driving later.

She took command of the music. When I heard the first notes of Prince's "Let's Go Crazy," I grinned at her.

"Dearly beloved," we said at the same time and laughed.

One of the things we bonded over as teens was music, and Prince's *Purple Rain* album had been played in heavy rotation.

"You got the lyrics right," I teased her.

A siren with a beautiful voice, Gianna's talent with music ended with the lyrics. She often sang the wrong ones, typically making zero sense, much to my enjoyment.

Gianna raised her hand and hollered, encouraging everyone in the bar to sing along with raucous enthusiasm. Many joined in. Who could resist a half-siren's song?

Once we settled back at the bar, I nursed my drink while we caught up. A Bon Jovi song played followed by Joan Jett.

Gianna turned her focus to one of her favorite topics—men. "You don't have anyone in the city? Not even a hook up?"

"Nope. If I had your cravings, I'd have starved a long time ago."

"Months?" she repeated in a louder tone.

Technically, over a year. "Shh," I attempted to quiet her, although I doubt anyone heard her over the music. In a lower tone, I admitted, "It's been so long that I've let nature take over down there."

Gianna's mouth dropped open. "Oh, no, no." She shook her index finger. "You need to rectify both of those situations right away. Let's start with getting you a profile set up online."

"What? No way," I protested. "My attempts at online dating varied between sitting through awkward silences or zoning out boasting blowhards. Most of the time, I'd rushed back to my apartment, eager for a bath with a book—or a more exciting date with my trusty ol' vibrator."

Gianna laughed. "Hope it's not old and rusty."

"No." I gave her a proud smile. "I treated myself to a good one."

She tapped my shoulder. "I'm glad, but still, the real thing is much better." Her eyes gleamed with excitement. "And next week, we're having a speed dating event at the club. Supes, humans, a smorgasbord of man flesh. After you find a hot hook up, I want to hear all about it."

Ah, the effects of being friends with someone with siren blood. She loved sex, and when she wasn't having it, she loved to talk about it.

"Sorry, Gianna. I don't plan to be around that long."

She sighed. "Still, you must scratch that itch before body parts fall off from lack of use." With a glance between my legs, she said, "Next up, the other problem. Which do you prefer, wax or laser?"

I crossed my legs, suddenly self-conscious about the forest down under. "I had one attempt with waxing myself. It didn't go well."

"Laser it is." She typed some things into her phone.

"Wait—what are you doing? I'm in town to take care of a *house*."

"And you need to take care of your *temple*." She glanced up at me before continuing typing. "You're all set with a free consultation in two days."

"Hey," I protested. "I didn't agree to that."

"It's with Sadie," she continued. "She's the best. Just go for a quick visit and hear about the options."

I groaned. "What are you getting me into?"

"Reminding you to take care of yourself. Someone has to." With a decadent smile, Gianna added, "Besides, you'll be happy after you remember how good an orgasm feels."

"I haven't forgotten." I raised my chin. "Remember my battery-powered friend?"

She sipped her drink. "You've neglected your needs for too long, Nova. While you're in town, I'm going to help you get back in the game and enjoy yourself."

I arched my brows. "By burning the hair out of my flesh?"

Gianna laughed. "Once you remember what it's like to be with a partner again, preferably one who knows what he's doing, you'll be smiling."

I exhaled. Maybe she was right. After all, I was still in my mid-twenties. Too young to give up on love, despite my lackluster attempts. My parents' bitter divorce hadn't helped me believe in a happily ever after. They still quivered with rage when they hear one another's names. But a lover would warm my bed much better than a cold battery-powered device.

"I don't know. Maybe."

"No maybes." She shook her head and tapped on her phone some more. "If you're still around next week, you're in for speed dating. If not, I'll cancel."

"Jeez." I rubbed my temples. "I haven't seen you for more than half-an-hour and you've already signed me up not only to have the hair burned from my body, but then to parade said body at a meat market."

She smiled with satisfaction. "Efficient, aren't I?"

I exhaled. "I can't argue with that." No Doubt's "Just a Girl" began to play. I bit my lip. "Will the laser hurt?"

"Yes."

"Oh!" I leaned back in mock horror. "Then why are you signing me up?"

"Because it's worth it. I barely have to deal with hair removal anymore."

"I should go before you think of something else crazy to sign me up for next. Thanks for the drink." I stood.

"You sure you don't want to stay longer?" Gianna asked.

"No, it's been a long day. I'm pretty much ready to go home and crash. I want to get up early tomorrow and start figuring out what I need to do with my aunt's apartment." Shaken, I'd left soon after Diego tackled me.

"Okay. I'll be home late. I'll try not to wake you."

"I picked up a couple of bottles of red so I'll probably have a glass or two before I go to bed and will hopefully sleep like the dead."

As soon as that word left my mouth, I thought about Diego—technically the undead.

She raised her chin. "Good luck tomorrow."

Luck? Would I need it?

DIEGO

As I sat in the living room on Monday, my gaze kept wandering from my historical fiction novel toward Margaret's apartment. Nova was over there.

"Still want a taste?" Sebastian asked from the kitchen where he was stirring the batter for biscuits to go with the beef stew cooking on the stove. The scent of cooking meat and spices filled the room.

"What?"

"Nova's blood."

Oh. I snapped my focus back to the book, regretting telling him about the surprising craving yesterday. "Don't be ridiculous."

"Then why do you keep looking over there?"

"Wariness," I quipped. "Let's not forget she almost killed me yesterday."

Sebastian wagged a finger. "Ah, I know you better than that, Diego. Your nostrils were flaring like she was fresh baked garlic bread dripping with melted better." He raised his fingers to his mouth and smacked his lips together.

I shifted my position in the leather recliner. "She smells good. I'll give her that. So what?"

"So we'll see," Sebastian added in a knowing tone.

I fought the urge to walk over to him and double-slap the smirk off his face.

"There's nothing to see." I scowled.

"If you're into her, just man up and ask her out."

I arched my brows at him. "You want me to ask out my landlord who might be getting ready to evict my ass?"

Sebastian laughed. "It wouldn't be as weird if you're not her tenant."

"This whole situation has strange stamped all over it," I countered.

"How so?"

"I'm a vampire."

"Oh, I didn't know that," Sebastian teased with a laugh. "I'm a shifter. Nice to meet you." He extended his hand as if we were meeting for the first time.

"Funny."

"It kind of is. You're good looking, she's hot. What happens when two people are attracted to each other is that they sometimes hook up."

I drummed my fingers on my thigh. "Not as much as you, my friend."

"What can I say? All this testosterone makes me a dog." He stirred the pot. "But when I find my mate, things will change. Wolves are the most loyal of all." He grinned a Cheshire smile. "Until then, I'll have my fun."

"I bet you will." I reopened my book, reading the same page for the third time. After I still hadn't followed the words on the page, I gave in to the distraction. "Besides, she's not interested."

"You sure about that?" Sebastian's eyes twinkled.

I'd seen that look on his face before, which meant he was up to something. "Whatever you're thinking, planning, or plotting, the answer is no."

"I'm not thinking of anything," he protested.

His mock innocent expression didn't fool me. "I don't date for a reason."

He dropped his head back and groaned. "Oh no, you're not going to say Diana, are you? That was over a year-and-a-half ago. Practically ancient times."

I groaned. "Well, she stole my life, broke my heart, and made me one of the undead. Stuff like that tends to damage a guy."

"If you look at it that way." Sebastian took off his apron and grabbed a bottle of beer from the fridge. He raised it. "Why not reframe it like she gave you immortality? You're lucky not to worry about dying like the rest of us."

"Which makes the idea of being with any mortal even less appealing. Why would I want to be with anyone knowing they're going to be gone one day?"

"You're friends with me. I won't live forever." He took a swig of beer.

"That's different."

"How?"

I put the book down as reading it was clearly an exercise in futility with Sebastian's incessant dogging. "I don't know, it just is. Maybe because we're not in a romantic relationship."

"You don't think we've got a bromance going on here?" Sebastian teased.

"Abso-freaking-lutely not."

Minutes later, Lucas returned to the house holding a Clash album. "I'm going to keep that place in business."

He loved to collect albums, and when a new record store opened nearby, he found a new place to spend all his one-dollar bills. He played the album on the record player and *London Calling* filled the room.

Nova entered the kitchen, her hair in a loose braid pulled to one side again and tendrils falling down around her face. "It smells delicious over here."

"I'm making beef stew and biscuits," Sebastian declared with pride. "You should join us for dinner."

"That would be great," she said. "Actually, I was coming over to ask something." She glanced at the floor.

"What is it?"

She raised her gaze. "Did my aunt…" She shifted her stance. "Did she die in her bed?"

I felt for her. How discomforting this situation must have been. Since I was the one who'd found her, I spoke up. "No." I'd found her on her bedroom floor, but wouldn't provide any of the details that Nova didn't want to know.

"Oh." She rubbed between her eyes. "I was just thinking. There's so much to do over there, and I'm already so tired. I have a feeling things will take longer than I expect. I don't want to crash at Gianna's for too long and overextend my visit…"

When she didn't finish, I said, "So you're thinking of staying there?"

"Is it weird?" She scrunched her face as she searched our reaction.

"Not at all," I assured her.

"It's your house now," Sebastian added.

Nova slanted her head. "Oh, good. I don't know the protocol in this type of situation. I'd like to take a nap and then get back to it."

Lucas said, "If you need a hand with anything, we're close by."

"Thanks." She rubbed her forehead. "I don't even know where to begin. There's all her clothes. And knick-knacks. And magical supplies in the attic. What do I do with all this stuff? Donate it? I'd like it to go to people in the community who need it most." Before waiting for an answer, she added. "And there's the paper-work. Figuring out what needs to be done with the house is just a mind warp of confusion."

She appeared overwhelmed. Another pang of empathy hit me. "We know the house well, so we can help," I volunteered.

Sebastian exchanged a glance with me and gave a subtle nod.

"You'll help me?" Nova asked.

"Of course we will," Lucas said.

"What can I do to repay you?"

"Don't worry about it," Lucas replied with an easygoing wave.

"It's almost time to eat," Sebastian announced. "Wash up and head to the dining room."

Lucas laughed. "Okay, Dad."

We sat around the oval table with our bowls of stew, biscuits, and a chianti. Sebastian overfilled my bowl as usual, and I poured half of it back. He'd never understand that my vampire appetite was not as voracious as his shifter one.

"This is sooo good," Nova said after swallowing a spoonful of her stew. "I can't remember the last time I had a homemade meal like this. Do you often eat together?"

"Only when we're not all working, which isn't that common," Sebastian said. "We're all working tomorrow night, so you had good timing."

"I'll say," she agreed. "This stew is delicious."

A few minutes later, Sebastian said, "Actually, I thought of something."

I stared at him as he used his *I'm-up-to-something* tone.

"About what?" Nova asked.

Exactly what I wondered, my wariness antennae raising.

"How you can repay us for helping with the house."

"Oh, how?" she asked.

"There's a ball this Saturday hosted by the Salem Supernatural Network."

"Oh yes, they told me about it," Nova said. "I wasn't planning on going, though."

"Why not?" Lucas asked.

"I won't know anyone there," she replied.

"You know us," Sebastian added with a grin. "And it might be good for you to meet some other supes while you're in town."

Why that would benefit her, I couldn't guess. Sebastian had his strange interpretation of how the world worked. I didn't say anything while I listened closely.

"Not sure it's a good fit for a talentless witch," Nova replied, and then took a sip of wine.

"You don't have to be skilled in magic to go to a ball," Sebastian replied.

"Right, just give it a go," Lucas added.

"I didn't bring anything to wear, but I suppose I could go shopping." She glanced at me as if waiting for my reaction.

"Can't hurt," I said—a man of many words.

Nova blinked a few times and then she tilted her head. "I don't see how this is repaying any of you."

Sebastian's smile widened. "I'm getting to it." He flashed a quick look at me before returning his gaze to Nova. "Here's the situation. Diego's ex is going to be at this ball, and he's not happy about that."

I glared at him. Why was he bringing Diana up? "I already told you I'm not going," I declared.

Sebastian raised his index finger. "But if Nova comes with us, she can pretend to be your girlfriend."

Was he insane? I raised both hands. "No way."

Sebastian pointed at me. "Calm down, drama king. Hear me out." After I nodded, he said, "Eventually, you're going to run into Diana again. You might as well be prepared for it." He gestured in a circular motion toward me and then Nova. "Knowing her, she's likely to be there with a guy."

True. I swallowed the bitter taste that coated my tongue. Diana was man crazy, which I'd learned the hard way. One guy just wasn't enough.

"Having a hot woman at your side shows her that you've moved on," Sebastian added.

"What do I care what she thinks?" I replied with a dismissive shrug.

"It will be good for you," Lucas added. "It's better than staying in these four walls or going to work, which is all you do. These balls are fun." He laughed and added, "Not as fun as mine."

"Jeez, Lucas. Female company." I glanced at Nova.

She appeared unscathed and smiled. "After living in a co-ed dorm, I'm familiar with the male fascination with their own anatomy."

"So what do you think, Nova?" Sebastian prodded.

She bit her bottom lip. "I don't know. I mean, Diego and I barely even know each other. How would we even begin to pretend that we're dating?"

"He's a guy. You're a girl," Lucas explained with a decisive clap. "I'm sure you two can figure it out."

Nova stared at the table. She then raised her gaze to meet Sebastian and Lucas's before dragging it to mine. "Sure, I guess I could do it. If you're up for it, Diego. Helping each other out and all." She shrugged. "No big deal."

Our eyes locked. My insides turned as stone hard as a gargoyle's as my unbeating heart seemed to echo in my ears. Her cheeks turned pink, and she glanced away.

"No big deal," Lucas repeated with a mile-wide grin.

To me it was a colossal one. Facing the woman who'd deceived me had as much appeal as eating dirt. Sebastian's insane idea did have one upside, though. If Diana was there, it would be easier to face her by having a someone as hot as Nova at my side. It would show her that I moved on, even if I couldn't declare with certainty that it was true.

"So we're all in agreement." Sebastian slapped his hands on my thigh.

"Sure," I agreed and then immediately felt my gut churn.

What the hell had Sebastian gotten us into?

CHAPTER 4

NOVA

What a day. I'd started by wandering through my aunt's apartment, taking an assessment of what she had, and what I should do with it, and ended agreeing to pose as a vampire's girlfriend.

When I returned to the room after dinner with the guys, I gazed in bewilderment at all the stuff. Apparently, my aunt wasn't into the Marie Kondo technique of decluttering that had led me to clean out a good portion of my belongings last January, only keeping what "sparked joy." Since I didn't know where to begin, it was overwhelming.

The room on the main floor was mainly a sitting area. It had a light blue sofa with a lounger at one end and an impression left in the cushion where she might have spent many hours. She didn't have a television, but had stacks of books in the bookshelves built in between the windows of the circular room. Her reading taste was eclectic, from books on science and nature to fiction of all types. Colorful Tiffany-style lamps provided lighting. Plants hung from every wall and almost every surface. They appeared to have been recently watered, which was good. Some framed photos were also strewn around the room and on a desk —photos of my aunt and other women, whom I guessed were friends.

Before I opened any shades, I made sure the door to the other side was locked to avoid repeating that incident with Diego. When I opened the ones upstairs in her bedroom, sunlight streamed into each window of her bedroom. In the center of it was a queen-sized bed with lilac-colored sheets and a white down comforter. Light purple was prevalent in her wardrobe as well as the color of the house, so I guessed it to be her favorite color. Her closet and white dresser were stuffed with clothes a size bigger than me. Touching her personal things made me feel strange, but I'd have to deal with it all, eventually.

Her workspace on the top floor left no doubt where she practiced magic. An altar with an athame, wand, and salt was set before one of the windows. Bookshelves were stuffed with tomes on witchcraft and magic and numerous small glass jars filled with herbs and who knows what. Just staring at some old leather bindings left me near spellbound. More photos in small frames were set about the space. One in particular stood out—it was my aunt holding me as a toddler. She had a wide smile on her face. Another one included the two of us holding hands. I was older in this photo, maybe four. It raised more questions. Why had she once been a part of my life and then poof, gone?

By the time I'd met up with the guys and Sebastian had invited me for dinner, I'd been thoroughly overwhelmed. There was so much *stuff.* It was kind of them to offer to help, and I'd do my best to take them up on the offer. Yet the payment in return was utterly strange. Agreeing to go to the ball and pretend to be

Diego's girlfriend would be weird. He was quiet and intense. One part of me found him cold and aloof, another part found the mystery fascinating.

Maybe after a good night of sleep I could think more clearly.

Before I settled in for the night, I changed the sheets. In a closet, I'd found another light purple set, this one with a plaid design. The sense of impropriety remained. Could I sleep here? My aunt had died in the house. I didn't know exactly where and didn't want to find out because that would add to the creepiness.

To unwind, I read a book. The mystery I had been reading wouldn't help with my nerves, so I bought a light romantic comedy on my e-reader.

When I was tired enough to sleep, I put the device down and turned out the light. My gaze traveled over the unfamiliar outlines of the bedroom and I stared into the darkness for too long. I tossed and turned with my eyes open for what seemed like hours before I finally fell asleep.

It seemed like no time had passed when I awoke with a jolt and sat upright. My heart was racing. Was there something in the room with me?

Or someone?

I turned on the light and scanned every inch of the room. Nothing stood out. Yet something was there. I could feel the creepiest of sensations slithering across my skin.

My breath came quick, and goosebumps crawled up my arms. I tried to move, but couldn't. I was frozen.

No. That couldn't be possible.

I attempted to call out for help, but my lips wouldn't move. Fear clutched every nerve.

Was I awake? Or was this some sort of nightmare brought on by my unease?

My gaze darted to every corner, and I kept alert for any sounds of movement.

Years seemed to roll past before I could move again. The statue-lock situation lifted, and I was able to move my limbs.

I climbed out of bed, rushing from the room in a desperate attempt to get out of there. My heart thundered in my skull as I sprinted out and down the stairs. I darted on bare feet into the shared kitchen. Fortunately, it had some light cast from beneath the stove hood.

After I reached inside the cabinet to get a glass of water, I closed it. A pair of bright eyes stared at me from the darkness of the living room.

I gasped and dropped the glass. It shattered on the tile floor around my bare feet.

"Hey, what's wrong?" a familiar man's voice asked.

The figure rushed closer to me, and I stepped back. It was Diego.

My heart beat louder than the bass that had been thumping through the club earlier. "What are you doing?" My voice came out at a high-pitch.

"Nothing."

"Wh— Why were you watching me?"

He squinted at me. "I wasn't. I just came home from work."

"Wait. What?" I was so confused that I didn't follow what was going on. "Were you in my room?"

Diego jerked his head back. "No. I'd only been home maybe two minutes, doom scrolling on my phone, when I heard you rushing down the stairs. I stood to see what was up."

I put my hand on my chest, and my heart pounded beneath my fingers. "You need to stop scaring me like this."

He blinked. "How did I scare you? I was sitting in my living room when you ran in. You startled me."

I bit my lip. He had a point. Maybe I was overreacting since I'd been so spooked.

"You're trembling." His voice turned gentle, and he touched my forearm. "Let's get you to the couch."

When I nodded and lifted my foot, he stopped me. "Watch out for the glass." He raised a hand. "Can I carry you?"

"Why?" My eyes bulged wide.

"I don't want you to cut your feet." He raised his chin. "All right, here we go—three-two-one."

Before I could protest, Diego scooped me up and carried me toward the sofa. The reality of my situation rumbled through me like an avalanche of mortification. Not only had I dashed over like a little girl scared of the dark, but I'd also shattered a glass, and had a vampire rescuing me from said broken glass. I glanced down at my Wonder Woman pajamas. Holy humiliation. I hadn't expected anyone to see me in my fun pjs, let alone Diego.

He placed me down in front of the couch.

"Thanks." I kept my gaze on the aged maroon rug.

"I'll go clean that up and get you some water." He handed me the remote. "Here, go nuts. Find something to distract you."

After I took it, Diego returned to the kitchen. He grabbed a broom and swept the broken glass into a dustpan. After he dumped it, he filled a glass with ice and water.

Was this the same sullen guy who had been so quiet throughout dinner? He was being considerate. And I had to admit, he was kind of cute.

Actually, more than cute. Although his blue eyes were intense, they now appeared gentle.

When he glanced over at me, he caught me staring. I quickly lifted the remote and flipped through channels. When I saw Hugh Grant and Andie McDowell in *Four Weddings and a Funeral,* I stopped.

Diego walked back into the living room. "Good choice." He handed me a glass of ice water.

"Thanks." I sipped the cool liquid. Nothing had ever felt so refreshing. I gulped half of it down.

He sat beside me, leaving a respectable foot or so. "Tell me what happened, Nova," he encouraged in a tender voice.

"I-I-uh, it's difficult to explain." I put the glass down on a Doctor Who coaster on the worn coffee table. "It was this feeling. A darkness that felt like it was smothering me. I couldn't move and was terrified. But then it passed and was gone." I faced him. "Maybe it was a nightmare—but I felt awake. No," I insisted. "I *was* awake."

The gentle expression in his eyes was comforting. "It sounds terrifying." He patted my thigh. "Don't worry, I'm nocturnal and will be up much of the night. You can hang out with me as long as you want."

I glanced down at where his hand had touched my leg. A strange heat remained. "I appreciate it." I still couldn't figure him out and pulled my legs up to my chest, turning to focus on the movie.

As Hugh Grant made social blunders and made them worse when trying to fix them, my own awkwardness seemed to recede. Diego even laughed at a few of the scenes with me.

Maybe this vampire was moody, but not so broody after all.

DIEGO

Although Nova had been tense when I'd carried her over in her adorable pajamas, she appeared to relax as we watched the movie. With her so close, I breathed in her aroma and a pang of hunger stirred. Fortunately, I'd had a pouch of blood earlier so the urge to drink hers was muted.

After a few minutes of focusing on the movie, Nova turned to me. "It's kind of weird what we've agreed to for the ball."

I groaned. "Sebastian and Lucas. They're too much sometimes." I steeped my fingers. "Don't worry, you can back out."

"No, it's fine," she said. "I'm happy to do so. Like I'd said, it's no big deal." After a pause, she added, "It's just a little strange. I guess I should get to know a bit about you."

"Sure, what do you want to know?"

"Umm." She glanced around the room. "Do you have family around here?"

"No. I grew up in Vegas. My parents are still there. No siblings."

"Do they—*know?*"

"That I'm a vampire?"

"Yes."

"No." I swallowed. "It's better they don't know." Becoming a vampire meant cutting off my family. Another sacrifice I'd made for what I'd thought was true love.

Nova nodded with quiet understanding.

When I asked about her family, she replied, "My parents divorced when I was a kid, and I'm not close with either of them. I'm also an only child."

"Where do they live?"

"My mother remarried a few years ago, and they moved to Myrtle Beach. My dad moved out west and has a new family. I haven't seen him since I was in high school."

Before I could ask her more about that, she turned the focus back to me. "What do you like to do?"

"I work as a lab tech at the clinic most nights and generally sleep until the early afternoons. From that point, I stay busy inside. Read, listen to music, go online, hang out with the guys, play video games, stuff like that. When the sun sets, I usually walk to work or at least get out for a walk."

"And if you're not working?"

"More of the same, really. I might go to the movies alone. I'm not big on socializing. The only people I really hang out with are the guys here. We sometimes go to a bar or to listen to live music. I prefer smaller clubs to big crowds these days. Too much stimulation."

"Ooh, I love going to shows, especially when the older rock bands go on tour." Nova brought her hands together. "Gianna and I bonded over music. So many musicians who didn't quite fit in found an outlet or a connection. It gave freaks like us hope."

I stared at her and nodded. "I know exactly what you mean."

Nova released a low breath. "Okay. We need to come up with our story. How we met and so on. I need to picture my life here."

"Sure. If you did live here, what do you think you'd do?"

Nova chewed her bottom lip. "Oh, I don't know. I mean it would be cool if I could still be working with getting books to kids, like I am now."

I cocked my head and studied her. "What is it that drew you into that field?"

Her lips parted as she gazed off into the distance. "That same ol' sense of being an outsider. I didn't have many real friends other than Gianna, so I'd escape into books. I could relate to the other outcasts and think, one day, my time will come."

I felt for her, relating to the sense of being alone all too well. "Has it happened yet in New York?"

She smiled. "I'm still working on it."

That meant she was still searching, like me. Our gazes locked. I sensed an understanding between us. We were both misfits. I was lucky to have found the Salem Supernatural Network and connected with Lucas and Sebastian, or else I might still be moping, searching for a place to call home.

I swallowed and tried to steer us back to safer ground. "Can you say that you work for the publishing house remotely?"

"Yup. I may have to pick up a few small assignments if I end up staying for more than a week, so it's technically true." She glanced around and her gaze settled on Lucas's record collection. "So for how we met, why don't we say at a rock show?"

"Sure." Since Diana knew how I liked live music, it was an easy sell. "Shared interest and all. Which band?"

"Hmm, the last concert I went to was The Cure—and they were *ah-may-zing*."

"Yes, I've seen them live," I declared. "And I agree. When they played 'The Forest' live, it blew my mind. Never thought it could sound that phenomenal."

"I remember them playing that," she agreed. "Did you see them in Boston?"

"No, it was at least five years ago, when I lived in Vegas. I only moved to Salem a year-and-a-half ago."

"Ah." She tapped her index fingers together. "Maybe we should say we met at their concert in Boston."

"That works." That question might never come up, but at least we had a story if it did.

We shared more about each other, even delving into topics that would likely never come up, such as our favorite colors—hers blue, mine forest green.

Nova was easy to talk to, and I enjoyed getting to know more about her.

She crossed her legs and then uncrossed them before she leaned forward. "I should probably ask what happened with you and your ex, if that's okay."

The good times threatened to crash to a halt. My tongue thickened and an acrid taste filled my mouth. "Yes, that makes sense."

She adjusted in her seat. "Oh, it seems like it's not something you want to talk about."

"It isn't, but you're right, you should know," I clarified. Before I came off as morose once more, I spat it out. "We were engaged."

Nova slanted her head. "What happened?"

I ran a hand through my hair and exhaled with a whoosh. "Perhaps I should start at the beginning."

Her eyes were wide and full of understanding as she waited patiently for me to continue.

"I met Diana almost three years ago and was instantly smitten. She was worldly and beautiful and glamorous. I couldn't believe someone like her would dream of being with someone like me —even if she was a vampire. I was utterly naive. Because I believed in her and I believed in us, no matter what the cost." I snorted. "In some romantic delusion, I agreed to become immortal to be with her." One hand curled into a fist. "A colossal mistake."

"We all make mistakes."

"But sometimes the toll is life-changing." With a sour snort, I added, "In my case, life ending."

She slanted her head and asked, "Is that why you became a vampire? To be with your ex?"

"Love sucks. Yeah, Yeah." I sang my variation of the J. Geils song.

"Sounds like it," Nova agreed. "What happened with her? Did she just walk away?"

I pictured her leaving with her new lover, the familiar pain cutting into me. "Yes." The back of my neck tightened, and I stretched the muscles to each side. "She told me she loved me and that it would be us against the world." I shook my head. "Nope. I was one of many. She had other lovers whom she strung along. Others whose hearts she broke. It's like she thrives on causing anguish."

Nova was quiet for some time before she pushed her shoulders back. "Screw her, Diego. She sounds like a heartless nightmare. She took a lot from you, but we won't let her take anything else. We'll show her that you've moved on and she didn't break you." Nova's expression appeared full of determination and hope.

My voice caught when I spoke. "But what if she did?"

Nova exhaled and covered her heart. "Then you find a way to put yourself back together."

Nova's optimism stirred a lightness in my chest. Could she infuse me with hope? I feared it might be too late for me. When she fell asleep beside me on the sofa an hour later while we watched the movie, her chest rose and fell in long, slow movements. In sleep, she appeared younger and more relaxed, so different from that haunted expression she wore in the kitchen. It didn't help that I'd scared the crap out of her—again.

Sebastian was right. I really needed to work on my social skills, especially around her.

For the moment, I was content to just sit beside her while the movie played. She might wake up confused about where she was—or have another terrifying nightmare—so I'd stay nearby to make sure she was okay. I'd seen the film a few times and didn't have to pay attention to the plot, which was good since my focus was on Nova.

Shadow, Lucas's cat, came downstairs. He often joined me at night since I was the only one up.

After petting him, I glanced at Nova. Was she cold? I reached behind myself as slow as possible to grab an afghan. I covered her, moving slowly, so as not to disturb her, and then relaxed into the sofa cushions.

Nova was turning out to be far different from what I'd expected. What did I think exactly? That she'd be a hotshot from New York who'd parade into the place and act like she owned it, which technically she did? That she'd only look at her inheritance with a cool eye focused on her financial gain? She wasn't like that at all. Somewhat overwhelmed by the situation, she still wanted to do what she could to help others—even me.

How did she survive in the city without those sharks eating her alive? Maybe she was tougher than I thought.

Then again, I'd seen her in her most vulnerable state as she'd stumbled in the kitchen, shaken, and then my unexpected presence terrified her. I now wanted to soothe her fears and take away her distress.

Wait a minute, why was I thinking this?

Just because she'd agreed to pose as my girlfriend for one night didn't mean anything. We were just doing each other a favor and would soon be out of each other's lives.

Yet, that drive of wanting to watch over her continued until the early morning hours. It stirred something inside I hadn't felt for a long time—caring for another person. It felt good. It gave me a flicker of hope that I could be more than just an animated corpse taking up space.

Could someone as damaged as me find purpose in the world?

Nova stirred. I moved from the couch over to the recliner so as not to freak her out when she woke and found me beside her.

I glanced at her. Could someone like her ever care for someone like me?

Nope.

I shook my head, an attempt to knock that foolish idea loose. Why even have a mad fantasy that a woman who was only in town for a short time would ever be interested in a vampire?

CHAPTER 5

NOVA

I woke in the early hours of the morning on the sofa in Diego's apartment. He sat in the arm chair, reading a book by the light of a lamp beside him.

What a night. I pulled myself up. "Sorry I fell asleep here."

He put the book down. "Not a problem at all."

I shuffled back to my apartment and curled up on the couch. Ugh, I'd acted like a kid afraid of the dark.

But it'd felt so real.

Diego had been considerate, though, with making sure I was okay. He'd calmed me enough that I'd fallen asleep beside him while watching the movie. This guy confused me on every level, not only with his behavior but my reaction to him. Something about him lured me in. And after finding out about what his ex had done to him, I was even more resolved to help him face that bitch.

Hours later, I awoke and checked my phone. A text from Gianna read *Don't forget about laser today. Make sure you shave all the parts you want treated.*

Shit, yes, it was Tuesday. I opened my planner and saw the appointment noted with an Edvard Munch *Scream* sticker.

I thought it was just a consultation.

You might as well try it while you're there.

I groaned. Freakin' Gianna.

Why the hell had I agreed to physical torture? I had enough to deal with while I was in town. I could blame it on the alcohol and Gianna's pushiness, but I'd only had one drink.

Oh well, if laser minimized dealing with hair removal as part of my beauty regime, it would be worth it.

Wish me luck, I texted Gianna.

Good luck, she replied. *Don't worry. You'll be happy you did this when it's all done. You'll be as sleek as a seal!*

That doesn't sound very sexy.

She replied with a laughing emoji.

The point is to get you groomed before you go out there on the prowl again.

Another thing I was not looking forward to. Hmm, I'd only been in Salem a couple of days and thus far I'd almost killed my vampire tenant, had agreed to pose as his fake girlfriend, signed up to pay for the pain of having hair lasered of my body, and possibly being roped into some freaky ass speed dating event.

After I pulled up beside the white brick building and found a metered spot on the road, I went to face step one of getting my groove back on.

I entered and descended to the basement level where there was only one door. Once I stepped inside, I entered a small waiting room, decorated with the standard white walls, chairs pushed to the edge of said walls, and a table with magazines spread on display. It seemed like a hole-in-the-wall salon. I swallowed my reservation and told myself to believe Gianna. After all, it didn't have to look like some fancy boutique to do the job properly, right?

"I'll be right there," a woman's voice called out from behind the partially ajar door.

I sat in one of the chairs and picked up a magazine on a side table, absently flipping through it. Before I flipped past the ridiculous amount of ads, a blond woman, who appeared to be around my age, walked out of the room and extended her hand.

"You must be Nova, Gianna's friend," she said with a warm smile. "I'm Sadie."

"Yes, that's me." I glanced at her, quickly assessing her for unruly body hair. If I worked in a place like this and had access to a laser, I'd zap every unwanted hair off my body.

Anyway, Sadie didn't have a stash or unibrow. Anything like that would make me question her abilities.

She motioned for me to follow her into that room she stepped out of. "We can talk in there."

Once I stepped inside, I sat on a cushioned seat. I glanced around the wall, scanning a poster depicting the stages of hair growth, and then the bloodthirsty machine that fed on unwanted hair.

"Have you ever had laser hair removal before?" Sadie asked.

I mashed my lips together. "No, and I am a little scared."

"That's natural. Most people are. Many report that it doesn't hurt as much as they expect."

"I hope you're right."

For the next several minutes, Sadie described hair growth and cycles. She explained the risks, which made me wrinkle my nose. Who wanted permanent scarring? But, that was rare, she assured me. She then described the different packages and promotions they had, starting with six visits several weeks apart. What? I wasn't planning on being in town that long. Gianna knew this. Did she have some ulterior motive to have me come back to visit town more often? Or think I would stay?

I chose to go for armpits and bikini line today, but insisted on only one visit, explaining how I didn't expect to be in town long. Then again, the house situation could require more visits. Whatever, I'd deal with it then.

"Laser away," I said with a flourish of my arms.

Several minutes later, I lay on my back wearing nothing but a hospital robe. What was it about these flimsy materials that made me feel even more vulnerable? All my confidence vanished to a layer as thin as the fabric.

Sadie put on some cream to help desensitize me.

"I hope it numbs me," I said. "I don't want to feel a thing."

"It's not that strong," she said. "You will feel a slight burning sensation."

My face scrunched up. That did not sound like fun.

"Where do you want to start first?"

Underarms or bikini? Neither body part stepped up to volunteer.

Time to suck it up. "My underarms." At least I wouldn't be naked for that part.

Deep breath, deep breath. Women do this every day. Stop being a wuss.

Sadie gave me a pair of odd yellow glasses to protect my eyes and she put on a similar pair. Now everything was masked in a strange amber hue.

She adjusted things on the machine. With each second that passed, my anxiety rose.

Sadie held the white device in her hand and stepped to my side. "Are you ready?"

"Yes," I replied quickly while nodding like a bobble head.

"If you need me to stop, just say so." She approached my armpit with the device. A strange red light flashed, an odd noise sounded, and I recoiled at the sudden jolt. It was like a baby dragon had crawled into my arm and exhaled fire.

"Eeeyoch!" That odd and somewhat mortifying squelch escaped me before I could suppress it.

"Are you all right?" Sadie asked.

"I'm okay." My cheeks burned after that mortifying squeal. "It was just surprising as I didn't know what to expect." I forced a smile. "Now I know."

I resumed the position of bracing myself, and she pressed whatever button it was that inflicted the torture. The baby dragon lashed out again in its temper tantrum. I forced myself to stay statue still, warning that spastic reactions could end up with me being scarred for life.

In every aspect.

Light, sound, burn. Light, sound, burn. When would it end? Armpits were small, yet they never seemed so humongous as she worked her way through every last hair.

After a thousand ice ages passed, she said, "All done with that side." She moved to the other one.

Ugh, we were only halfway done. And only with one procedure.

I told myself that it wasn't that bad. Another voice piped up to say, *yes it is. Not only that, it will get worse. Think about the lady parts getting burned.*

No flipping way.

What the hell was wrong with Gianna for suggesting this? How did any woman on earth sign up to endure this willingly?

I was *not* any of those women.

Sucking it up, I braced myself to endure the other underarm. After all, I couldn't leave hairless on one side and sasquatch on the other.

When Sadie praised me for doing so well, a lie she probably told every client, she said, "Let's move on to the bikini line."

Burning hair near my sensitive lady parts. Courage leaped out of my body and bolted from the building. I raised my arm. "Sorry, I can't do it."

"Are you sure? Why not try it and see? You've done so well."

More lies.

I pressed my lips together. "I just can't." Humiliation tumbled forth as I babbled, "I'm sorry, I'm more tense than usual. I had a strange nightmare last night, and maybe I'm still rattled."

It was a lame ass excuse that sounded even more absurd as it came out of my mouth.

Sadie cocked her head. "What did you dream about?"

That was odd. Most people weren't interested in other people's dreams. "It wasn't really a nightmare because I'd swear I was awake…but… more of a dark sense of being smothered by this, I don't know, shadow. It seemed to weigh on me. I couldn't move."

Sadie stepped back and covered her mouth. "No way."

Another odd reaction. Ah, what was it about Salem that drove people to act whack-ass weird?

"Yeah." I wrung my hands together. With a sheepish shrug, I added, "I guess I just want to explain why I'm acting like such a freak."

Her eyes widened. "It's strange because my friend told me the same exact thing happened to her two nights ago." Sadie nodded with a knowing expression. "I thought it must have been sleep paralysis. She was pretty freaked out by it, too."

"Oh." My nerves pinged like I'd been struck by ice. Why did this revelation make whatever happened a thousand times more menacing?

"This can't be a coincidence," Sadie added.

Those words shocked me as much if she still had the laser aimed at me. "What do you mean?"

"It sounds dark." She arched her brows. "And it sounds like more than a dream."

Words failed to form, as if my voice box had been zapped.

Several minutes later, I left without my pride, but at least my crotch hadn't been attacked by a torture device. With a nervous laugh, I attempted to shake off the spooky vibes that clung to me after hearing Sadie's ominous words.

At least, I had taken the step to groom down there again, not that I had plans for anyone to see the results anytime soon. I pictured Diego and his sexy bedroom eyes, but then shoved that image away. That would only complicate my time here.

I pulled out my phone and called Gianna. "Are you trying to kill me?"

She laughed. "That bad?"

"It was like I was thrown into a tank of sharks with freakin' laser beams."

"Easy, Dr. Evil," she replied to my Austin Powers reference. "You got through it, right?"

"I most certainly did not." I hoped my indignant tone masked my sheepishness. My bruised and burned ego didn't agree.

"Seriously?" Gianna asked.

I pursed my lips before admitting, "I made it through the armpits, but gave up at bikini line."

"Come down to the club tonight, but don't drive. I'll make you something potent so you don't feel a thing."

Best suggestion I'd heard since I arrived in town. Besides, I could use one before explaining to Gianna all that had happened since last night.

Maybe she should make that drink a double.

DIEGO

When I went downstairs that afternoon, Sebastian and Lucas were hanging out in the living room both absorbed in their screens. Sebastian stared at his laptop, and Lucas at his phone.

"Hey, have you seen Nova?" I asked in a forced nonchalant tone while I brewed coffee that I'd spike with some B positive blood.

Sebastian glanced up. "She left this morning to run some errands."

"I think she's back now," Lucas added. "Why?"

Ignoring him, I asked, "How did she seem?"

"Fine, I guess." Lucas cocked a brow and flashed a knowing grin. "Once again, why?"

I ran a hand over my jaw. "I might have startled her last night."

"Again?" both said almost simultaneously.

I blew out a harsh breath. "Not intentionally. I'd just come in from work and plopped on the couch. She came into the kitchen to get some water. When she saw me in the dark, she dropped the glass."

Lucas chuckled. "That's so you to lurk in the shadows."

I pointed to my eyes. "One of the perks is stellar night vision." I bent down to see if light reflected on any pieces of glass I missed. "Watch out for broken glass in here. I swept it up, but you know how sneaky those shards can be."

"You weren't your sullen-ass self, were you?" Sebastian asked with a wary expression.

"No," I protested. "I was friendly. We watched a movie."

Sebastian narrowed his gaze. "*You?* And her?"

I rolled one shoulder. "Yeah. What's the big deal?"

One side of his mouth curled up into a grin. "Is something going on with you two?"

"Of course not." I snorted. "You know that." When Sebastian and Lucas exchanged a glance, I added, "Don't do that."

"Do what?" Lucas asked.

"The look. Nothing is going on," I protested.

"Then why is your tone all weird?" Sebastian added.

"My tone is not weird." As soon as I said it, I heard what he meant. Not only was my voice louder, but more defensive. "Forget it," I dismissed. "I'm going to make sure she's okay."

As I walked through the kitchen, they snickered.

The door to her place was closed. *Don't say anything that comes off as creepy. You've already done that enough.*

I knocked on the door. When she said, "Come in," I made sure the shades were drawn before I entered. No need for more embarrassing entanglements.

"Hey, Nova." I leaned against the door frame in a relaxed posed, feigning nonchalance.

"Hi, Diego. What's up?" She was curled up in one of Margaret's afghans on the sofa, reading some papers in a manila folder.

When she caught my gaze, my breath seemed to get stuck somewhere in my throat, which was strange since I didn't need to breathe. My position then felt more forced than natural. I stood up straight.

"Just wanted to see how you're doing." I motioned toward her. "You know, after last night."

She closed the folder and set it on the coffee table. "I'm not usually so on edge. Sorry about breaking the glass and making a mess."

"No, it's fine." I took a couple of steps into the living room. "I get it. You're in a new place with strangers. All of this has been thrown on you. I'd be wary, too."

She bit her lip and didn't respond for a few seconds. "Can I ask you something?"

"Yeah, sure."

She shook her head. "No, never mind. It's nothing."

"No, tell me," I encouraged.

She smoothed the afghan over her legs. "Okay. Please sit." She motioned to the off-white armchair across from her. Once I did, she said, "I was at an appointment today."

"With the lawyer? Realtor?"

Her expression turned perplexed. "No, nothing like that. A women's appointment."

"Oh." That could mean a whole realm of things I wouldn't understand.

"Somehow the nightmare or whatever it was came up. The woman I was talking to said the same thing happened to her friend two nights ago. *The same thing.*"

"Oh," I repeated, proving my mastery of the English language.

"That's super weird, don't you think?" Nova asked.

"Yeah, I guess. Who was this lady? A witch?"

"I don't think so. It was a... um... beauty appointment." She pulled the afghan up higher. "What do you think? Have you ever felt a dark presence here?"

I snorted and then pressed my hand on my chest. *"I'm* usually considered the dark presence in this house."

Nova flashed me a you-know-what-I-mean look.

I leaned forward, placing my hands on my knees. "No, I haven't sensed anything like that."

She tapped her lips and glanced around the room. "I'm thinking of going back to stay at Gianna's."

"Why?" My voice definitely came out louder than I'd planned.

She hunched her shoulders before rolling them back with a sort of shudder. "What if it really was something? If so, I don't want to sleep in that bed again tonight."

"Listen, Nova, you don't have anything to be worried about in this house. I'm here. I mean, we're all here. If there's anywhere you're protected, it's with three supes."

What was I doing? Why did I care whether she slept under this roof or at her friends' house?

"True," Nova agreed with a nod. "Maybe it's just anxiety."

I stood and offered her my hand. "Then we'll just have to do something fun to distract you."

She tossed the afghan aside and took my hand. "Like what?"

Since it was daylight, I couldn't leave the house, but we had plenty indoors to keep us occupied.

"How about a game? We have video games in the living room and board games in the basement."

"Ah, the basement. I walked through the other day. I saw a bunch of musical instruments as well as things I know nothing about how to operate, like the heat and hot water systems. I quickly retreated upstairs."

"I might be able to help with any questions." I took her hand before leading her to the stairwell off the back of the kitchen. The touch of her skin on mine sent strange, warm tingles radiating inside me. I released my hold before we reached the final steps.

The basement was semi-finished in the main area with storage boxes and the washer and dryer. I had my drum set down here, Sebastian had his bass, and Lucas his guitar.

"Do you play any of these?" she asked.

"The drum set is mine. The three of us played together for a while, and we learned to play some rock songs, but we don't do so that often anymore."

"Do you play on your own?"

I grinned. "Not as much as I should."

"You should," she encouraged, touching my arm. "I have zero musical talent, but envy those who do."

These days, I typically only played when I wanted to get out of my head. It was good for stress release. Ha, I should probably come down and pound on the drums to help deal with this strange attraction to Nova. I needed all the help I could get to get her out of my system.

I led her to one of the shelving units with the board games and puzzles. "Lady's choice."

She glanced at the stack. "How about Scrabble?"

When I carried the box upstairs, Sebastian piped up. "I want to play."

"Me, too," Lucas added. "But our way."

"How's that?" she added.

"Much more fun," Lucas replied.

Sons of bitches. They were creeping in on my time with Nova.

Maybe that was for the better, though. Being alone with her last night had already stirred such a confusing reaction. Their presence might help keep me grounded—especially since they'd call me out if I started to make an ass out of myself.

"Instead of following boring rules," I said, "We make up our own words and have to provide a convincing definition."

"Ooh, that sounds fun," Nova replied. "How do you figure out who wins?"

"The teammates vote on whether they'll accept. I mean you can't put down a string of consonants and some half-ass description. You need to put some thought into it. And honestly, we don't even care who wins. It's more fun just to mess around."

We played the game, and Nova fit right in.

When she spelled out *zalor*, Sebastian prompted, "What in the world is that?"

"A snowy owl that lives in Canada." She raised both hands as if it was common knowledge.

"Good one," I praised. I built off her Z with Zong, a character from a Dr. Seuss book, which I sold as a "type of fishing boat."

We continued making up nonsense words until all the tiles were used and Lucas won. Or cheated. Whatever. It didn't matter. I had to admit it was fun with the four of us.

After the game ended, Sebastian and Lucas headed into work.

Nova glanced at the clock. "I should get back to house stuff."

"I can give you a hand," I offered. "I don't have to go into work until later tonight." Jeez, could I sound any more eager?

We tackled some boxes in the basement until she'd had enough for the day.

"We could watch a movie," I suggested.

"Sure." She tilted her head and gave me a warm smile that shot shivers of delight through my body. "I picked the movie last night, so it's your turn."

"I'm in the mood for something feel good, that's easy."

"What?"

"Anything by Monty Python." Her blank expression showed no recognition, so I followed up with, "You've *never* seen Monty Python?"

She wrinkled her nose. "I don't think so."

I placed my hand on my forehead and sighed with melodrama. "She hasn't seen Monty Python." Turning back to her, I asked, "Dead Parrot? The Ministry of Silly Walks? The Spanish Inquisition?"

"Doesn't ring a bell." With a sly grin, she added, "I must have been waiting for a hot vampire to introduce me to it." Her eyes widened, and she clamped a hand over her mouth. "Oh, frick."

It was too late. I heard it, and a lightness filled me. I pumped my chest out. "You think I'm hot?"

She shook her head. "Forget I said that. That came out way too flirty."

I laughed. "Don't worry, I think you're pretty damn hot yourself."

"Thanks." Her cheeks darkened to a shade of pink, making my fangs itch to come out and play. Fortunately, I'd drank blood earlier. After the initial reaction to her scent, I made sure I was well fed before I saw her.

After searching through the options for Monty Python, I said, "Those are some great skits." I scanned some more. "Oh, but the movies. So good."

"Just pick one you like," she said.

Longer would be better as it would give me an excuse to spend more time with her. "A movie." I finally suggested *Monty Python and the Holy Grail.*

I pressed play and settled back against the cushions, relaxing my shoulders so I wasn't as stiff as a corpse in a coffin. I kept a respectable six inches or so between us, yet remained keenly aware of how close she was beneath the blanket and how good she smelled. Her fragrance reminded me of sunshine and roses after a summer rain. How could I not want to warm my face under the heat of the elusive sun, an experience I would no longer have?

As soon as she saw the actors clapping coconuts to simulate the sound of horses clopping, she turned to me with an amused expression. "This is ridiculous."

I smiled. "It's only the beginning."

As the movie progressed, we chuckled as more silliness played out on screen. Somehow, we ended up leaning against each other, our thighs touching, and my leg burned with awareness.

When the Rabbit of Caerbannog took the stage, Nova didn't just laugh, she leaned her head back and howled. She wrapped her arms around herself and tears flashed in the corners of her eyes. "A killer bunny?"

I grinned. "The Rabbit of Caerbannog."

After the credits rolled, she glanced at me. "How have I never seen this before?"

"Exactly," I replied with a knowing look.

She placed her hand on my forearm. "Good call. You'll have to introduce me to some others."

The pleasant warmth beneath her hand drew me to glance at it. When I raised my gaze, I locked on hers and couldn't pull away.

I didn't want to. My palms heated and a buzz of awareness simmered in my veins.

Her lips were right there. So close. And so perfect. They were pink and plump and shiny. All I had to do was lean closer and I could…

Nova took in a shaky breath and turned away. She pulled her hand back.

The moment was over, but the heat of her touch lingered.

WHILE I WAS at work later processing blood tests in the lab, I thought about Nova. Although I told her we'd be there to watch over her, I wouldn't return until my shift was over before dawn.

What if she had another incident while I wasn't around? Sebastian or Lucas might be there to comfort her. An unexpected pang of jealousy struck me at the thought of them being alone with her, and I cringed. I needed to stop thinking like this. Whatever this perplexing attraction I had for her had to go.

Then why on my break did I order her a stuffed killer rabbit online, thinking it would be a funny housewarming gift—a cute reminder of our moment together?

I groaned. I'd just ordered a woman a stuffed animal of a killer rabbit with fake blood coming from its mouth as a gift. No wonder I was single.

I tried to force her from my mind after I returned home and slept.

That afternoon, while I was preparing a blood protein smoothie, Nova entered the kitchen. She appeared as pale as a Scandinavian vampire. I turned off the blender.

"Oh, Diego. Good, you're here."

"What is it?"

She stared at me with haunted eyes. "I sensed it again."

"Sensed what?"

"The dark magic."

The words didn't come right away. When they finally did, I uttered my kick-ass go to line. "Oh."

After I blinked and kicked myself to say something else, I added, "What did you sense exactly?"

Her mouth slanted down as her expression turned grave. "I don't think my aunt died of natural causes. She was murdered."

CHAPTER 6

NOVA

How had I not sensed it before? The cloying scent clung to my aunt's belongings in her bedroom like a pungent perfume. It was so pervasive that I doubted it would ever come out, like how smoke clung to fabric.

"How do you know?" Diego asked, his blue eyes wide.

I chewed my lip before I could pull my thoughts into words, still shaken by the encounter. "While I was gathering dresses to donate, I smelled this faint odor. It grew stronger. And then—it sounds weird, but it felt like ribbons slithering around me. Even though I couldn't see anything, I ran from it, scared it might capture me and leave me unable to move, like the other night. I ran out of the bedroom and shouted *stay* before I shut the door behind me and bolted down the stairs." It sounded insane even to me, but it was the second time something unexpected and somewhat unexplainable happened to me over there. "It appeared to stop chasing me. And somehow I knew—*I knew*—

that it wasn't a dream the other night or my imagination. It was dark magic, and it had killed my aunt."

Diego's mouth fell open. He turned even paler than his already vampire white. "Do you think it was trying to hurt you?"

My bottom lip trembled. "I don't know."

"Damn. We need to check it out. Let me get the others."

I touched his forearm. "Why, what are you going to do?"

"See what's going on." Diego's expression turned determined.

I kept my hands on him. "But what if you get hurt?"

"Don't worry," he assured me. "I'm supernatural."

I wish I had his courage.

Once Diego gathered Sebastian and Lucas, we walked back to my aunt's apartment together, me clinging to Diego's arm.

The pungent scent made my lips pucker. "There it is. Awful, isn't it?"

Diego sniffed. "I don't smell anything." He glanced at the others. "You?"

Lucas shook his head and muttered, "Nope."

Sebastian's nostrils flared. "Nothing. And a wolf has an acute sense of smell."

This didn't make sense.

Diego opened the door, and I sucked in a breath.

"Be careful." I held onto him with both arms. The scent wasn't as powerful as it had been, but it still lingered. "Do you smell it now?"

"No," they replied one after the other.

I couldn't believe it. "How can I, a talentless witch, smell it, but you three supes with phenomenal senses of smell, can't?"

They all exchanged glances before Diego fixed his gaze on mine. "Maybe you're more gifted with magic than you realize."

As the hours passed by, I questioned what I'd been so certain about. Why would I sense dark magic and not them? Why had I been so certain my aunt was killed by it?

Still, there was no way I would stay there tonight. A raging desire to sell the house and be rid of this mess rose, but I couldn't even do so at this point. Not with all that remained to be done.

And could I in good conscience sell a house with dark magic to someone else, saddling them with a problem that could kill them?

Nope.

"Since we can't help you figure out what it is," Sebastian said, "You're better off finding someone who can."

"Like who?" I asked.

They all looked at me as if waiting for the answer to become clear—and it did. "Right. A witch."

"Fortunately, you're in the right town to find one," Lucas said with an encouraging grin. "Home of the Salem Supernatural Network." He stood. "Hold on."

He went into his bedroom and returned a minute later with a business card. "I worked with a witch named Colleen. She has a store right here in town."

"Thanks." I had Lorna LaRue's number, but she was a lawyer. Maybe this Colleen would know more. I made the call and explained how I wanted to talk to someone about a problem, she replied that she had an open appointment at noon tomorrow.

"Is it urgent?" Colleen asked. "If so, I can connect you with someone else."

Although inside I screamed yes, was it truly an emergency? I started to wonder if my perception was off. "I'm not sure. I sensed dark magic, but my roommates didn't. But I don't have any magical talent." As I explained it, more doubts surfaced. Maybe I'd imagined the entire thing after all despite how real I'd convinced myself it was.

"Okay, we're a little backed up with so many calls at the moment. Stay out of the area for now and keep the doors closed. If anything changes and you need someone sooner, call back immediately."

After we ended the call, I summarized what happened to the guys. "I have an appointment tomorrow. She told me to stay away from the space, so I'll stay at Gianna's tonight."

"You sure?" Diego asked. "Our sofa folds out into a sleeper."

He was sweet. I couldn't believe how wrong my first impression was. "Thanks, but I think I could use a breather. I mean, just knowing what's over there." In a smaller voice, I added, "*If* I didn't imagine it."

"Of course you didn't imagine it," Sebastian added.

"Now I'm not sure." A wave of foolishness washed over me. What if it had all been caused by anxiety again? Maybe I needed to see a shrink rather than a witch. "I'll know more once I talk to her." After I exhaled, I said, "Guys, I don't know what's going on, or if I can trust my thoughts, but please be careful. If you sense any threats, get out and call the network right away."

The more time I spent with them, the more I liked them. I hoped I was wrong about the whole dark magic thing as I couldn't stand the idea of them being in danger.

Especially Diego.

"That is messed up," Gianna said after I got her up to speed with all that had been going on.

We sat at the bar of Danger Zone while Samantha Fox's "Naughty Girls Need Love Too" played. Each of us drank a glass of the house red wine they'd named *A Vampire's Caress.*

I thought of one vampire in particular and how it would feel for him to caress me and then shoved that thought aside.

"Do you think I could have made it all up?" I asked her.

Gianna took a sip of her wine and put down the glass. "Honey, I have no idea. The only person who can answer that is you."

"That's the problem. I was so certain when it happened, but once I started to think about it, I second-guessed myself."

"Never do that, Nova." She pointed at my chest. "You need to believe in yourself."

That was a problem rooted way back in childhood. Maybe I should see a shrink instead of a witch.

"Thanks for letting me stay at your place again. Once I talk to a witch, maybe my nerves will settle. It's ridiculous how spooked I've been since I returned to Salem. It's like I haven't spent the last couple of years in New York becoming desensitized to all the weirdness." Then again, Salem had its own brand of peculiar.

"Stay as long as you want." Gianna gestured around the club. "I'm here most nights, anyway." After taking another sip of wine and a scan of the male clientele, she returned her gaze to me. "Have you thought about sticking around longer?"

"Not really," I replied. "Actually, the incident made me lean more to the idea of selling and soon."

I HUNG around Gianna's apartment until it was time to leave for my noon appointment with Colleen. I walked down to a stretch of retail businesses in a brick building near the waterfront where I found the store. Witch globes and crystals hung in the window, twinkling in the sunlight. After I entered the store, a songbird of wind chimes announced my arrival. Sunlight streamed in through the glass. Various displays were set up on tables and shelves at different levels—one with herbs, another with Tarot cards, another with silver jewelry, and so on.

A young woman with blonde and lavender ombre hair and Goth makeup looked up from the herb display she was restocking. "Hi, there, can I help you find something?"

"Hi, I'm Nova Adams. I have an appointment with Colleen at noon."

"Right over there." She motioned to a woman by the cash register with curly blonde hair who appeared to be in her forties.

"Welcome," Colleen said. "Let's go into the back."

I stepped around an orange tabby cat and followed her through a colorful beaded entryway at the back of the store and into a small room. She closed the door, and I glanced around. A bookshelf was stacked with books, a crystal ball, tarot cards, a bamboo plant, and more trinkets than I could count. A round table had three chairs set around it and a dark blue velvet tablecloth on the top. Another set of tarot cards was half-covered by a burgundy velvet wrap.

"Have a seat." She motioned to one of the chairs. After I did so, she sat and asked, "Tell me what the issue is."

I told her about inheriting a house from my aunt.

She clasped her hands together. "I know Margaret well." She frowned. "Knew." After shaking her head, she said, "I'm so sorry," and clucked her tongue. "Such an unexpected tragedy."

"Yes, indeed," I agreed.

Colleen tipped her head. "Oh, I've heard of you. You live in New York, right?"

"Um, yes." I crossed my legs. It was downright strange to have this stranger know about me. Then again, just about everything since I'd stepped back into Salem was downright peculiar.

"Are you in some kind of trouble?" Her expression turned concerned.

Would she think what I was about to say was crazy? After taking a deep breath, I admitted, "I sensed dark magic in the house."

She nodded, encouraging me to continue.

I clasped my hands together. "The first time, I thought it might be a nightmare, but I know I was awake." I mentioned how I'd heard of it happening to someone else, as well, although it sounded like a story about a friend of a friend. "But yesterday, it was much more vivid and coming for me. I had the distinct feeling that whatever this presence was killed my aunt."

A flicker of wariness appeared in Colleen's pale eyes, but then it was gone, and her face was impassive once more.

I leaned back in the chair and released a nervous laugh. "Hearing me say it out loud to a stranger makes me sound like a nut."

"Not at all," Colleen said. "It's been… eventful lately."

"How so?" I tipped my head.

"Too much to get into right now, but we've been overextended dealing with similar reports."

"Oh." I frowned. "Does that mean I should be worried?"

"Not if you take the proper precautions," she said.

"Meaning?"

"You need to clean all traces of dark magic from the house."

"Wait—you don't want to investigate?"

Colleen sighed. "I'm familiar with what you're referring to. We've been finding traces of it all over the area. If we weren't so overextended, I would come, but there's nothing that I can do that you can't yourself. Your house is well guarded with layers of protection. Since it's your house, it will be more effective if you perform the ritual."

"But, but," I stammered. Raising both hands, I said, "I can't do it."

"I'm sure you can. It's basic magic." She pulled a booklet off the shelf. "Follow these instructions on how to clear all the negative energy."

"No, you don't understand," I explained, "I can't do magic at all."

She furrowed her brows. "Excuse me?"

"It's true. Not even a basic spell."

Colleen stared at me as if I had tea leaves on my forehead she was trying to read. "But I sense magic in you."

I leaned back and shook my head. "You must be mistaken. I'm telling you. I'm hopeless."

"Interesting." She clucked her tongue.

I gave her a sheepish grin. "Maybe it skips a generation."

Colleen followed with a crystal-ball type of gaze at what I guessed was the position of my third eye—not that I'd ever considered even having one until that moment. I squirmed under her probing stare. Should I extend my hands so she could read my palms next and complete the full body scan?

"I don't think that's it." She clapped. "Tell you what. Try it. It's easy to follow, and I think you can manage. If I'm wrong, call me."

Although I wanted to protest some more, what could I do—beg her to drop everything after she'd just mentioned how busy she was and to deal with my problem?

Unease crawled up my spine. The last time I'd played with magic returned to me like an icy cold slap, only what followed had been fire. Vicious and destructive fire.

"I—I can't." My hand trembled, and I hid it on my lap under the table.

Colleen appraised me with a long look. "Okay, I'll squeeze in a quick visit tomorrow and see what I can do."

"Thank you." Quickly, I silently implored. No need to sound hysterical. Besides, she'd said how crazy things had been lately.

What exactly did that mean? And what was causing it?

After I paid and left the magic shop, I walked toward the water rather than heading straight back to my aunt's house—or my house, rather, for now at least. It was weird to consider myself an owner of anything, let alone something as grand as a house. Funny how life could change in a bang as shocking as an unexpected firework.

Down at the shore, I inhaled the sea breeze. Toddlers toddled on chubby legs near the ocean's edge, filling up sand buckets as their parents stood nearby. Seagulls called from overhead, practically begging humans to throw them a freakin' French fry.

Despite all the weirdness, a part of me enjoyed being back here. Life was less hurried than the one I had in Manhattan. I told myself that it was what made the city great, the liveliness and the energy. The city truly never did sleep.

Maybe it was time to slow down the hectic pace, at least for a little while.

But how? The only true connection I had here was Gianna. Sure, I liked the guys in the house, but they were likely to pass out of my life soon, especially if I sold the place. We'd have no reason to see each other. I learned that through college and my time in New York. People came in and out of your life. Even those who were regulars for a period would disappear, eventually. Poof. Just like magic.

After a deep breath in which the sea scent seemed to invigorate me, I continued meandering through the sand. Maybe I was at a turning point in my life. The big question was, which way should I turn?

No way would I step foot in my aunt's apartment again until the dark magic was gone. At Gianna's, I made some calls and checked my work email to make sure nothing urgent had come up.

That afternoon, I went to the house to meet Colleen. It was already Thursday, and the week was flying by. Although I didn't think I would need a week in this city, now even two didn't seem long enough.

After I entered the kitchen, I spotted Diego in his living room watching the news.

"Hi Diego. A witch is coming at two to help me."

"Come hang out," he said. "It's just me. The others are out."

I sat on the sofa and caught up on the day's doom and gloom, but must have glanced at the clock at least fourteen times. Two o'clock came and went. I tried calling Colleen, and it went right to voicemail.

Disappointed, I stood to leave when the phone rang. It was Colleen.

"I'm sorry I can't make it. Something has come up."

I swallowed. "Oh, that's too bad." Now what would I do? "Can you come later?" My voice lilted.

"I don't know. A lot is going on." Before I could press for details, she said, "Don't worry, Nova, I'm certain you can handle this. All you have to do is try." After a pause, she added, "You *must* give it a try."

"Must?" That was weird.

"Please," Colleen insisted. "I need to go."

After she ended the call, I blew out a breath and plopped back onto the sofa. Shit. That sucked. I had to put on my big girl panties and try some magic. Something I had no desire to attempt again.

Diego asked, "What's wrong?"

"She's not going to make it. She told me to try to clean the dark magic." I pointed to my chest. "Me," I repeated with emphasis. "She doesn't realize how much of a bad idea this is."

Diego cocked his head. "Why?"

Tightness griped my throat. I dreaded telling the story, one in which I questioned what was actual memory or filled in by my speculation. Yet, he'd confided in me when telling me about Diana. "It's a long story." I shook my head. "Actually it's not since I don't remember much of it. What I do is in fragments and pulled together from what I heard."

"Memories can be tricky that way," he said in a gentle tone.

I brought my hands together and took a deep breath. "I was around five and tried to do a spell. Nobody knows which one, and I don't remember." Struggling to keep my voice steady, I tried to tell the story of fractured memories from a distance, as an observer. "But whatever I did sparked a fire. It was small at first. I called my mom and rushed from the room. Before I made it out, the fire raged, and then smoke filled the room." My nostrils flared at the acrid scent in my memory, and my pulse quickened. I took some deep breaths to slow my racing heart before I continued.

"My mom shrieked when she saw the fire, picked me up, and ran. I remember choking on the smoke as we rushed to get out of there. Clinging to her in terror as I gasped for air. Thinking we were going to die. And then I passed out."

Diego took my hand and squeezed it. "I'm sorry, Nova. That experience must have been terrifying."

I nodded, squeezing back tears. Sobs threatened to rack my body, but I held them at bay.

When I was ready to continue, I said, "I woke up in the hospital and didn't speak for almost a week. My parents fretted over me and forbade me from ever doing magic again. They told me how dangerous it was. I believed them. Not only had I burned down part of our house, but I almost died in the process. So I didn't try it for years, not until I was in high school and feeling a bit rebellious. I knew other witches. If they could practice magic, why couldn't I? But I tried a few spells with them and poof—nothing." Fixing my gaze on Diego's blue eyes, I explained, "Whatever I did that day when I was five had to have been a fluke. Maybe it wasn't even magic at all, but something I did accidentally. Now you see why I can't do magic." Waving my hands to the sides, I added, "At all."

Diego gave me a sympathetic look. "It's possible. But there could be another explanation."

"Like what?"

"Not sure. But you said Colleen sensed magic in you. You're an adult now. Why not give it a try?"

I shook my dead. "I don't know, Diego. I'm scared."

"I'll stay with you. I won't let anything bad happen."

The sincerity in his tone made me believe him.

"Do you want to try?"

Skiing naked during a blizzard sounded more appealing. "Not at all, but I have to give it a shot." With a half-smile, I added, "Besides, it's my responsibility as a landlord to keep my tenants safe." Gazing into his eyes, I asked, "Will you really stand by me?"

Diego nodded, his gaze boring into mine. "Of course."

A tingle of heat danced through me. "Okay, let's do it."

CHAPTER 7

NOVA

The booklet that Colleen gave me wasn't much more than a no frills list of ingredients and steps to clear negative energy from a location. She'd included a bundle of sage in the bag.

Having Diego there gave me the courage to face returning to the apartment. After all, he was a vampire. Who better to have with me when facing darkness?

After bracing myself, I reentered her apartment. Shadow, the gray cat, followed us, but stopped outside of the bedroom door and hissed. He ran back down the stairs.

I sensed dark energy as clearly as if it had been spelled out with scratch marks into my skin. The oppressive negativity appeared to grasp for me like shadowy tentacles, but I continued up to the workspace on the third floor with Diego right behind me.

On the altar, I found a small gold bell, one of the items I was looking for. "I'm going to start with this." I took a few deep breaths as directed to center myself and focus on my energy. After the anxiety from rushing up here dissipated, I envisioned casting my circle within this room.

I lifted the bells and rang them, walking in an ever-widening circle. "I banish all negative energy from this space. The darkness will be driven away by light. I will fill this home with positive energy and cast my intention to do so."

Although I felt foolish for doing this, Diego didn't regard me as such. His expression held encouragement, not judgment. After I set down the bells on the altar, I lit the end of the dried sage. I found an amber stone and held it in one hand while I spread the smoke of the burning sage throughout the room as I continued the circle and repeated the words. As I did, I pictured the negativity being pushed out by the smoke. On the third go round, I felt the power in the words. It was no longer just me repeating words. I felt the magic in them.

I lit a match and held it toward the wick of a candle, but then paused. A moment of hesitation grabbed me. After all, I'd literally be playing with magic and fire, an almost fatal mix when I was five.

When I glanced at Diego, he said, "It's going to be fine, Nova. You can do this."

His belief in me helped chase away my doubts. I exhaled and then lit the candle. On the third circle of the room, I repeated the chant, envisioning the light of the candle forcing away the final vestige of darkness. When that was complete, I faced Diego. "I think we're done up here."

"How do you feel?" Diego asked.

My body didn't feel so weighed down by anxiety, and my muscles weren't clenched so tight. I gauged the room. The energy seemed lighter as well. "Better. I think it did something."

"That's my girl," Diego said with a proud smile.

I glanced away as my cheeks turned pink. Why did his praise affect me so?

"Diego, I need to open the shades to let the light in. Can you move somewhere safe?"

"I'll wait in the stairwell."

After I ensured he was out of range of a sun death ray, I opened the shades. Light streamed into the room, illuminating the space. I stepped closer to the window and let the brightness warm my face. It felt exhilarating. I thanked the elements and then gathered the items I'd used in a bag. I'd need them to face the bigger challenge of the darkness in my aunt's room.

We descended the stairwell and entered the confining space. The darkness seemed to permeate each crack in the room, searching for places to hide, and I shuddered.

"You've got this, Nova."

This time I felt the power in Diego's words. His belief in me amplified my ability to conquer the darkness in this room. It could have all been in my head, but I didn't care. It invigorated me with bravery to continue. A magical tingling seemed to glow and spread inside me, extending out towards the walls of the room. I repeated the process to cleanse the area until all the darkness and negativity had dissipated.

I faced Diego and smiled. "We're done here."

Diego cocked his head. "Two down, one to go?"

I nodded. "Exactly."

After he was safely out of sun range, I opened the shades to let the light illuminate the room, casting out whatever was left of the darkness. We descended to the main floor.

On the third attempt, the steps came to me from memory. Compared to the bedroom, this process went quickly.

When I completed the final ritual, I blew out the candle. "Thank you." I walked counterclockwise and thanked the elements before closing the circle.

Since I didn't sense any of the darkness on their side of the house, I didn't think we needed to cleanse over there. The negative energy seemed to concentrate in my aunt's bedroom, but I'd extended the cleansing to the floors above and below to capture all of it.

The magic inside still lingered with a potency. It was electrifying, making me feel more—alive. I couldn't believe what I'd accomplished. Me, a hapless witch, had cleared a house of dark magic.

"We did it!" I declared.

"*You* did it," Diego said.

"I couldn't have done it without you." I threw my arms around his neck and hugged him. "Thank you."

The press of my body against his flooded me with heat and awareness. I pulled back and stared into his eyes, captured by them.

"You're welcome." The proud elation of his expression morphed to something else. Hunger.

My gaze remained locked with his, breasts against his hard chest. He moved his focus to my mouth, and my lips parted. My breath came quicker, heart thundering with anticipation.

I stood on my tiptoes as I closed the space between us. My lips brushed his. Although I wanted to melt against him, feel every inch of his body against mine, a voice in my head screamed, *what are you doing?*

"I'm sorry." I stepped back and glanced away. Why the hell did I do that? I had no business kissing my tenant. It had to be the high of successfully performing magic for the first time spurring me to be bold. "I got swept up in the moment, but shouldn't have done that."

When I summoned the courage to meet his gaze, he appeared conflicted. "No worries. I get it."

I exhaled with a shudder. We had the ball coming up on Saturday. Would I be able to dance with him and pretend to be his girlfriend without remembering how good it had just felt to be in his arms? That whisper of a kiss ignited a yearning for more.

"IT WAS A TERRIBLE IDEA," I told Gianna.

We were in the women's section of a department store at the North Shore Mall, shopping for an outfit for me to wear to the ball tomorrow.

Gianna searched through a rack of dresses in my size with the finesse of someone who knew exactly what she was looking for. That was good, since I didn't have a fraction of the fashion sense and style that she possessed.

"You kissed him, so what? You're both clearly attracted to each other. No big deal. It's not as if you slept together." She winked and added, "But you should."

I should have expected her reaction. She could be right. Maybe I was overthinking the whole thing. But it didn't seem right to kiss one of my tenants while I was in the process of figuring out what to do with the house. Why add any complications?

I had spoken to a real estate agent that morning, and she was going to come by to look at the house on Monday. A part of me felt guilty about doing so as it would affect the guys, but it wasn't as if I owed them anything, right? I mean, I liked them, for sure. I enjoyed hanging out with them. And Diego—well, I wasn't sure how to interpret my strange attraction to the vampire.

My desire did not seem unrequited. The way Diego glanced at me with hunger left me flush. Whether it was for my body or my blood, I wasn't certain, but the hunger in our kiss left me yearning for more. Why did I have any reservations?

We were both adults. Why shouldn't we hook up? If I sold the house, we'd never see each other again, so no strings would be attached. It would just be a fling. Why not break my dry spell with someone who'd made me feel more in his arms with a stolen kiss than any of the men I'd met in the past few years?

I pictured what it would be like had Diego and I continued our kiss and went into the bedroom. What would it feel like as he buried himself inside me? Would his fangs emerge? Would I let him bite me? I bent my neck and touched my throat. A dozen more questions followed. Would it hurt or feel good?

While absently flipping through a display of black dresses, I addressed Gianna, "Tomorrow is going to be weird."

"Why?" she replied.

"We're supposed to be pretending, but after that kiss…" I shook my head. Yes, I'd definitely complicated matters by kissing Diego. It was better to shuck off any ideas of anything more.

"This one," Gianna declared as she pulled a dress off the rack. It was a royal blue dress with spaghetti straps and a plunging neckline.

"I don't have the boobs to pull that off." I gestured at her. "We don't all have impressive racks like you."

She felt one of the bra cups. "Don't worry, it has some pads to enhance the girls. You won't even need to wear a strapless bra."

The dress was form fitting at the bodice and flared out with multiple chiffon like layers cut at various lengths at the bottom.

"Try it on." She handed it over. "It would look perfect with your figure."

That was the problem with me and shopping. Being on the petite side made it tough to find clothes that fit well. Dresses had to fit in a precise way to keep me from looking like a little girl playing dress up with her mom's clothes.

Gianna shooed me toward the dressing rooms. "Go, I can't wait to see it."

I went and tried it on, turning in one direction and then the other as I appraised the effect in the multiple mirrors. The chiffon layers swished around my legs as I twirled. I had to admit, Gianna nailed it. It was flattering from shoulders to shins, and the bra cups definitely drew attention to my breasts, displaying them to the point of almost overselling. Oh, well. Sex sells.

When I opened the door, Gianna smiled in triumph. "We have a winner." She clapped her hands. "*Please* tell me you like it. It looks amazing on you."

"I like it," I agreed, but then reassessed its suitability for the ball. "Should I add something to make it more fitting for Halloween?"

"We'll stop by the Halloween store and slap on a pair of wings to make you a fairy." She led me to the register. "Let's get lunch at the food court. I'm starving."

We picked up panini at a cafe. While we ate, I said, "I wish you were going tomorrow. It would be far more fun with you there."

"Of course it would be. But Halloween is one of our best nights, so I need to be at the club." She flashed the mischievous grin. "What I would give to see you and Diego pretending to be together in front of this vamp. Now *that* would be a show indeed." She took a bite of her sandwich.

Hell, I hoped not. The last thing I wanted was to make a spectacle out of us both.

"Next stop, a sexy pair of shoes," Gianna declared.

"I don't do well in heels," I protested.

"That's because you haven't found the right pair." She gave me a sage nod. "Don't worry, you're with me. If there's one thing I know as to what turns on a man, it's what turns on a woman —shoes."

I laughed. That definitely wasn't the case with me. "Then I might be frigid."

Forty-five minutes later, Gianna dispelled that theory when she found a pair of strappy silver heels that were sexy while also comfortable. I even managed to walk in them without stumbling.

She shrugged with false modesty. "What can I say, it's a gift."

DIEGO

"I can't believe you're making me do this," I told Sebastian as I walked by the bathroom.

He had the door open as he tidied his beard, something he did daily as part of his manscaping routine, which he insisted was a bitch to keep up with due to his wolf nature.

Sebastian rolled his eyes. "We're not going to go through this again. Just man up and do it."

I scowled before heading into my room to change. Tonight could be uncomfortable. While I searched for a suitable outfit, I questioned if Nova would even come. Had we made things too uncomfortable with that brief kiss?

Damn, I wished we could undo it, yet also fantasized about taking it further. No wonder I was so screwed up—my brain couldn't even settle on what it wanted.

After I found a decent pair of black slacks and button-down shirt, I took a shower and then dressed. When I walked to the stairs, I scoped the situation below. Nova was there. Lucas and Sebastian told her she looked great and asked her to spin around. She did so, twirling her dress. A set of white shimmery wings rested on her back. A growl rumbled in my chest.

Shoving away that unexpected pang of jealously, I drank her in. Her bright blue dress set off her auburn hair, which hung in loose curls over her shoulders and down her back. She had those tiny, wispy curls, whatever they were called, framing her face. She didn't usually wear makeup that I noticed, but tonight, her brown eyes appeared even larger with dark liner and mascara. And her lips, painted a lush red, drew my attention to her enticing mouth—one that I'd kissed two nights ago.

A rumble of need stirred inside as I remembered how good it had felt.

Would that ever happen again, or did she think it was a mistake? That we'd gotten caught up in the moment?

As I descended, Nova's gaze captured mine. Her scent filled me with the usual longing. My tongue seemed thick, and my mouth went dry.

I cleared my throat. "Nova, I wasn't sure you'd come."

"Erm…" she stammered. "I'm here."

Sebastian gave me a look I interpreted as *Get your act together, man.*

He was right—why had I said that when we'd had this evening planned? I ignored him and returned my focus to Nova. "I'm glad. You look beautiful."

She beamed. "Thanks. Gianna picked it out."

"She has great taste," Sebastian noted with an approving nod.

Lucas walked into the kitchen. "How about a drink? I made a batch of mojitos using the mint Margaret harvested at the end of the season."

A drink would help calm the nerves.

Lucas handed us each a glass of mojito crammed with mint leaves and toasted, "To Margaret."

After we repeated the words, I took a sip. The combination of mint and lime went down smoothly.

I needed it to keep me from sticking my foot into my mouth tonight. I'd need everything I could use to get through an evening facing the woman who had destroyed my life.

CHAPTER 8

DIEGO

The Phantom of the Opera played as we entered the hotel ballroom, which was fitting since the room could have stood as a set design, with all the ornate candelabras displayed on tables covered with black tablecloths. Fake cobwebs hung from the chandeliers and witches' pentagrams were prominent. Smoke wafted from punch bowls with blood-red liquid. Silver trays were stacked with appetizers that filled the air with the scents of baked cheese in phyllo dough.

"Looks like we stepped into a Gothic wonderland," Nova quipped.

Many in attendance wore black with silver jewelry, which was where I fell in, while others wore outlandish costumes. Lucas had picked a pirate outfit with his white shirt loose and unbuttoned, revealing a vast amount of chest. That was fitting since he liked to parade around like a peacock. He'd feed off the female attention tonight for sure. Sebastian dressed low key, like me, wearing all black, but unlike me, he wore a matching mask.

I turned to Sebastian. "See, I told you it wasn't a masquerade."

"It's staying on," he replied. "Ladies like the mystery."

He wasn't alone. At least a dozen others did the same. Some wore costumes begging to be noticed, like the couple who walked by in enormous black boots that must have given them six inches of height as well as another six inches from their curved horns. Whatever they were supposed to be dressed as was a mystery to me.

I searched for Diana. She didn't appear to be there yet. "Let's get a drink," I suggested. Liquid courage would help with my nerves.

Placing my hand beneath the fairy wings on Nova's lower back, I steered us to one of the bars lit up by red lights and covered in lacy black spiderwebs. Framed menus of what appeared to be blood-red writing on old parchment advertised specials like Medusa's Revenge and Poe's Punch. I didn't need the fancy marketing schtick and ordered a Chianti with B+. Nova ordered a Vampire's Kiss, a champagne cocktail colored red. I tried not to read too much expectation into it.

We wandered around the ballroom, sipping our drinks as we people watched.

"It didn't take them long." I tipped my head toward Lucas and Sebastian. They'd infiltrated a group of women bearing much skin in their tiny costumes.

"Is that usual for them?" Nova asked.

"Oh, yes." I took a sip of my drink.

"What about you?" She tilted her head and glanced at me with a faint smile.

"No. I don't go out much."

"Well, you are tonight. And I think we should make the most of it." After finishing her glass, she placed it on a tray on a table. "Let's dance."

"Oh, no," I protested. "I don't remember the last time I danced."

"Come on," she encouraged.

When she took my hand and nudged me toward the dance floor, I groaned and finished my drink. She led me into the middle of the crowd and moved her body to Stevie Wonder's "Superstitious." It was slow enough that I could just move through the motions without much effort.

Through the next few songs, I relaxed dancing with Nova. She was clearly enjoying herself as she danced to "This is Halloween" from *The Nightmare Before Christmas,* and her joy was infectious. When the Meteor's "Little Red Riding Hood" played, I alternated between spinning her around and pulling her in close. When I accidentally pulled her in too quickly, she bumped against my chest and gasped.

"Are you okay?" I asked, glancing at her with concern.

She stared up at me and her lips spread into a smile. "Never danced with a vampire before." She arched a brow. "I now know to be aware of your strength and speed."

I winked. "I'll tone it down to keep you safe."

The next song was L7's "Pretend We're Dead."

I joked, "I don't need to pretend," and she laughed. Seeing her happy encouraged me to continue. I loosened up around her and got into it.

People danced like zombies in Michael Jackson's "Thriller," and we joined in, chuckling at our increasingly ridiculous moves.

The DJ slowed things down with Frank Sinatra's "Bewitched," and I pulled Nova in close.

"Despite your reluctance to dance, you seem like you're having fun." Her cheeks turned rosy and so enticing. "Are you enjoying yourself?"

I hadn't wanted to come to this ball, but now I couldn't think of anywhere I'd rather be than dancing with her. We were having such a great time—better than any I could remember since I'd been turned.

Aware of our closeness and all the areas our bodies touched, from our joint hands to her breasts pressed against my chest, I had to swallow before I replied. "I am."

"I'm glad." She smiled, and it dazzled me. I couldn't tear my gaze from hers, losing myself in her hazel eyes.

As we swayed together, her intoxicating scent strummed through me, stirring my cravings. I longed to kiss her, to taste her blood, and to bury myself inside her. Hell, I wanted her. There was no denying it any longer. The tease of her lips on mine two days ago had haunted me with the yearning to kiss her again.

And do so much more.

Recognition flickered in her eyes as if she sensed my rising hunger. Her eyelids lowered, as she devoured me with a look of longing that mirrored my own. My gaze dropped to her parted, red lips, and desire pulsed in my veins. I bent my head toward hers in what seemed like achingly slow motion.

And then finally, my mouth was on hers. Her lips were warm, soft, and everything I wanted. Kissing her on the dance floor, I buzzed with a feeling that I hadn't had since I'd been turned. It was something elusive. Something I never thought I'd feel again.

Hope.

When we parted, her breaths came short and quick. Her expression was wondrous, as if she was just as dazed by that magical touch.

I searched for words, but none came.

Nova sighed. "It's so hot in here. I could use some air."

"Good idea," I steered us through the dancers toward the exit.

"Diego." It was a woman's voice, one I hadn't heard in so long, and I cringed. All the heat that had simmered through me while kissing Nova cooled like I'd stepped into a tomb.

My jaw clenched as I turned to face my ex. "Diana."

She stood beside a tall vampire with slick-backed blond hair and a pinstripe suit. She appeared as beautiful as always, statuesque and slim, almost a twin for Grace Kelly. Her off-white beaded flapper dress clung to her, revealing her slim limbs.

"You came." She brushed my forearm, and I resisted recoiling. Why did she have to touch me?

"I did." I ground my teeth.

"I'm so glad." She grinned her mirthless smile, which did nothing to brighten the mask of her neutral face. Nothing like how Nova lit up the room when she smiled. Diana was an ice queen through and through.

"This is Connor," she said.

I raised my chin in acknowledgment. A few silent moments followed.

"I'm Nova." She stepped forward and extended her hand. Both Diana and Connor exchanged greetings.

Inside, I groaned. I should have introduced Nova. What was wrong with me? The main purpose of her being my date tonight was for this encounter.

"Yes, this is my girlfriend, Nova." In a higher lilt, I added, "Or should I say, my fiancée?"

My gut churned with regret. Where the ever-loving fuck did that come from? Why had I blurted that out, stepping our fake relationship up another level without even mentioning it to Nova?

Her brows arched up in an astonished expression.

"I—uh—mean—well…" I stammered. Why couldn't a tidal wave sweep in right now and get me out of this mess?

Nova touched my bicep. "Oh, honey. You took me by surprise. I thought we were keeping it quiet for now."

At least she'd managed to come up with a reason on the fly for her shocked expression. Shit, shit, shit. Now I had to get myself together. "What can I say, darling? I'm excited and want to tell everyone."

Diana touched my hand, her cold fingers on me. Such a difference from Nova's warm touch. I resisted yanking my arm away and did so casually.

"Oh, Diego, that's wonderful," Diana cooed.

Did she think it was just as wonderful when we were engaged, and I promised her my mortal heart and soul?

"Is it?" I asked with bitterness and a cock of my head. Oh holy hell, I had to stop. Awkward silence was better than me sticking my foot in my mouth and following it up with a boot to the tonsils.

"Of course." She turned to Nova. "Let me see your ring. Diego has such good taste."

She would know—especially as she likely pawned off the one I gave her to gallivant with the next guy who came along. I bit those words back as something worse threatened to unravel my ruse. There was no ring.

"Oh, he most definitely does. I'd never seen a more perfect ring for me," Nova said. "But it's being sized right now. She raised her hand and moved her fingers about. "It's got to fit comfortably since I'll be wearing it til death do us part."

Not only had she covered my bumbling ass, but she'd lobbed a subtle zinger at Diana while doing so.

Diana's expression hardened, but she didn't acknowledge the barb. "Congratulations to you both."

Silent Connor echoed her statement.

I didn't even feel a modicum of celebration. I just wanted to get the hell away from Diana. "Excuse us, we were just about to step outside to get some air."

"Save a dance for me later, Diego," she purred.

Like hell I would.

As I rushed Nova to the entrance, I muttered, "Thanks for covering my ass."

All the elation from the night of dancing with Nova and then kissing her slowly crumbled away as my insides turned dark and twisted. Seeing Diana reminded me of the heartache, the boundless regret. I'd made the mistake of falling for a woman before, trusting her, and it had ended up destroying my life.

But Nova was different, nothing like Diana.

Oh shit, I had to get air and get my head straight. Nova and I were only here together as a ruse. If I put any hope of there ever being a real thing, then I was still the same dumb ass who'd been fooled by a vapid vampire two years ago.

NOVA

When Diana had stopped us, Diego's mood darkened as quick as a falling curtain. Not only had his expression soured, but the tension was palpable from his rigid posture. How different from the man I had danced with minutes before. He'd been relaxed and had a smile on his face, clearly enjoying himself. But when we kissed, passion simmered. Although we were in a room of hundreds, it seemed like it was only us. Our connection entranced me.

That was until Diana had interrupted and broken our magical cocoon. She was freaking gorgeous with perfectly styled, shiny, silvery-blonde hair that made me think of a mermaid. Not that I'd ever seen one or knew if they existed. The way she loomed over me with her statuesque, willowy figure made me feel like a troll next to an immortal supermodel.

Worse was how she affected him. I forced myself to stand tall and squeezed his hand for some moral backup. After all, when he'd stayed with me when I'd tried magic for the first time in years, his presence seemed to strengthen me. Could I provide the same comfort to him?

Not by his expression. He appeared lost, haunted—somewhere beyond where he could be reached.

Hell, I hated what she'd done to him. What I'd do to fix the damage.

Once we stepped outside the hotel, I asked him, "Are you okay?"

Diego's expression turned tormented as he stood statue-still beneath the full moon. Slowly, he pulled his gaze to mine, as if wrestling with an inner beast.

"Yeah, I'm okay now." He ran a hand through his hair. "It's been a long time since I've seen her."

"You did great," I said with an encouraging smile.

He exhaled with a shudder before one side of his mouth rose with a hangdog grin. "I thought I blew it by blurting out the whole fiancée thing. Thanks for covering my ass."

"Not a problem." I touched his shoulder. "How was it seeing her again after all this time?"

He snorted. "Like a punch in the scrotum." He shook his head. "How could I ever have fallen for someone like that?"

Not sure what he meant, I replied, "She's quite attractive."

He scowled. "She's as cold and impenetrable as a frozen lake." Wonder radiated from his bright blue gaze. "Nothing like you, Nova."

He pushed a tendril of hair off my cheek. "You're warm, like the summer sun." His eyes darkened with smoldering need.

"Oh, Diego." It's all I could manage to say. The intensity in his hungry gaze held my breath captive.

"You're everything she's not." He swallowed and tipped his head down.

My heart thundered with renewed anticipation. Before his lips met mine, the spell was broken by a woman calling my name.

After I pulled back from Diego, I searched for the source. "Colleen?" I was about to ask what she was doing there, but stopped myself. The ball was hosted by the Network. Of course she'd be there.

She glanced at Diego and then back at me. "Can we talk alone for a minute?"

"Sure." I glanced at Diego. "I'll be right back." Although I hated leaving him after the emotional torment left him so vulnerable, I couldn't blow Colleen off to say I was busy and about to make out with a vampire.

Once we stepped away from the hotel and into a nearby park, Colleen asked, "Were you able to clear the darkness?"

"Yes." I beamed with pride. My smile vanished when I glimpsed the worry on her face. "Why?"

"Nova, another witch has been killed."

My eyes widened. "What?"

"We've had so many troubling reports lately that we can barely keep up with the calls. Tonight, we learned of a mysterious death of a young witch. Dark magic was found at the site." She pursed her lips. "I should have come and investigated more when you'd reported it at your house. The Network had come to get her body, and I figured they would have picked up on anything that was off. And you'd seemed uncertain..." She planted her hands on her lips. "No time for regrets. I came to warn others, such as yourself."

I placed my hand over my mouth as my pulse escalated. "Oh, my. Is there anything I can do to help?"

"Yes, go home and shield your house and those inside with protective spells," Colleen directed.

My mouth fell open.

"Margaret placed many on the property around the house, but as the new owner, you should reinforce them with your magic."

I wanted to remind her of my lack of skills and that a simple bit of cleansing must have been a fluke, but she'd already disappeared into the mass of people inside the hotel.

While Diego drove us back to the house, I told him what happened. "We need to warn Sebastian and Lucas." Although only witches had been targeted so far, it still meant a murderer was in Salem.

He called Sebastian to fill him in, and I called Gianna. She didn't answer, so I gave her a quick heads up in a voice mail and asked her to be careful.

"The guys aren't that worried," Diego said with a shake of his head. "In fact, they said they'd met some witches and will be sure to go home with them to keep them protected."

"Probably a good thing."

Several minutes later, he turned into the driveway. After I climbed out of the car, I glanced around the yard, paying close attention to the shadows and bushes near the house.

"You okay?" Sebastian asked.

"A little spooked," I admitted with a self-conscious grin.

"Don't blame you." He searched the area.

With his vision, he'd likely see more than I ever could.

He placed his hand on my lower back and guided me toward the entrance on his side of the house. I exhaled. That was better than heading into my apartment alone.

One we entered, I stripped off my heels and the wings. Now what should I do? I threw my hands up. "I don't know how to cast a protection spell."

He pointed up to my aunt's apartment. "I bet you could find some tips up there."

Right, her workspace. It was full of enough magical supplies to stock a storefront.

Diego followed me upstairs. I scanned the bookshelves as I looked for something that might help.

"How about this?" He pulled out a dark blue hardcover that read *Spells for Protection* and handed it to me with a lopsided smile.

"Nailed it." I took the book and opened it. Wicked bats and flying monkeys, there were so many spells listed. Since it was me, I figured it was best to start with the simplest ones near the front of the book. I skimmed the table of contents. "Protecting your home and those within," I read aloud.

"A perfect match," he replied with a sage grin.

His expression turned more serious as he searched my eyes. Was he talking about more than just the spell?

Shaking that foolish thought out of my head, I turned the page for the spell I needed. The first part directed me to cleanse the space. Since I'd been able to accomplish that with Diego, I felt confident I could handle that part. I followed the steps to ground myself and then took a satchel of salt. "I need to go outside."

"What for?" he asked with a worried expression.

"I must spread it around the property line."

"I'm coming with you," he declared with determination.

No arguments from me. Diego stayed by my side as I followed the steps of the spell, spreading salt around the perimeter of the house as I walked barefoot over the grass. My feet were cold, but it was better to connect to the earth that way.

While holding hematite in one hand, I repeated a chant to protect the space and those inside. I took seven deep breaths beneath the full moon, envisioning myself drawing energy from the earth and extending it to the sky in a protective bubble. When I actually felt magic moving through me, I was stunned. Was I finally learning how to do magic after all these years? The house hadn't blown up yet, so that was a good sign. Lastly, I sprayed a mixture of lavender oil infused with various herbs and visualized it as another layer of protection.

After we returned to the house, I plopped onto the sofa in Diego's living room, noting how I'd spent more time there than in my aunt's apartment. It was comfortable to be with the guys —and more so with Diego. "Hope the spell works. It wasn't as difficult as I thought it would be."

He appraised me with a thoughtful stare. “You may be growing more comfortable with your magic.”

A week ago, I would have declared it was impossible, but I had managed to clear the house of dark magic and felt somewhat confident that this spell had taken root.

Shadow strolled into the room and jumped beside me on the couch. “Hey, sweet thing.” I rubbed his cheeks and under his chin, to which he responded with an approving purr.

“Drink?” Diego asked. “You earned it.”

“Sure.”

He returned a minute or two later with two glasses, his with a red tinge that had to be blood.

“Champagne?” I asked.

“Yes.” He grinned. “What did you have earlier—a Vampire’s Kiss?”

I had indeed, in more ways than one. Heat suffused my cheeks. “Yes.” Shadow jumped down to the rug and attacked one of his toy mice. I crossed my legs. “I think mine had grenadine to give it color.”

“The real thing is better.” Diego’s arched a brow.

Kissing a vampire was one thing. Drinking blood another. “I’ll take your word for it.”

After I took a sip of the champagne, I glanced over to my aunt’s apartment.

“What’s wrong?” he asked.

I flashed a sheepish grin. "Just wondering if I can work up the nerve to go sleep over there tonight. Or, if I should go back to Gianna's."

Diego cupped my chin and tilted it up. "Don't do either."

My breath caught in my throat as I stared into his bright blue eyes. They'd darkened a shade, capturing me with intensity.

His focus lowered to my mouth. He leaned forward and brushed his lips against mine. "Stay with me."

CHAPTER 9

DIEGO

When my lips met Nova's, the electricity zinged me. The chemistry was undeniable.

"Yes," Nova said.

Excitement roared through me. All that yearning that had built up in me from that night, burst forth when she said that one small word.

I hadn't planned to seduce her. What I had promised to do was keep her safe. Two witches had been killed in Salem. I didn't want to let Nova out of my sight if she'd let me watch over her.

As I kissed her, we moved up the stairwell. I drank in her sweet fragrance, almost tasting it on my tongue. The dance, the kiss, and all the heightened tension of the night had built up, and I couldn't stand another second without touching her. She stirred feelings in me I didn't think possible. The yearning to protect her drove me to predatory levels. I'd destroy anyone or anything that tried to harm her. I never felt so vulnerable as when I was around her.

Once we entered my room, I kicked the door closed and led her onto my bed. Her auburn hair tumbled over the bedspread, and she gazed up at me from under hooded eyelids. She looked incredibly hot tonight, but never so much as with her lips swollen and parted from our ravenous kisses.

I kissed her again and ran my hands over her body. My fingers traced over the exposed skin of her slim neck, her upper chest, and then over the fabric covering her breasts. A rumble stirred inside as I rubbed her nipples. They hardened beneath my touch. My nostrils flared as I scented her rising desire.

"Nova, you're so beautiful." I slid my hands down over her dress, slipping them beneath the hem to caress her soft thighs. "All I want to do is make you feel good. Bring you pleasure."

She sighed and encouraged me to continue with a small smile. "No arguments from me."

As my fingers edged up her thighs, I kissed the hollow of her throat. Her blood thrummed beneath her skin, drawing my fangs forward. It had been over a year since I drank fresh from a human, yet never with such sensual desire. Not only did I long to pierce her flesh and taste the sweet ambrosia, but I needed to thrust deep inside her.

Forcing myself to ignore the compelling song of her blood, I continued to follow the other urgent drives instead. My erection strained against my zipper, burning with the raging urge to enter her.

I kissed down over the top of her dress, trailing my tongue on the slight mounds of her breasts. They'd tantalized me all night, especially when we danced.

"Let's get this off you," I murmured.

When she arched her back, I unzipped her dress. We worked together to pull it over her head, leaving her in nothing but a black lacy thong.

I ran a hand over my mouth to regroup before I erupted right then. It had definitely been too long.

"Everything okay?" She stared at me with inquisitive eyes.

"Couldn't be better," I replied. "I just needed a moment because you're so hot."

She reached for me and unbuttoned my shirt. "I'm practically naked, and you're fully dressed." After she untucked it, she unzipped my pants. "I want to see you, too."

I pulled back to undress, quickly tossing my clothing to the floor so I could return to Nova. She drank me in with a bold gaze before murmuring a positive appraisal.

Careful not to crush her body, I lowered my weight onto her. It didn't take long for the passion to flare again as we kissed and touched each other with greedy hunger. I slid my fingers under the waistband of her thong and glided it over her hips, desperate to remove the last barrier between us.

Once we were finally skin-on-skin, I reached between her legs, stroking the soft folds. She was already so wet. I slipped one finger in and she moaned against my mouth as we kissed. Then I added another.

Soon after, she was panting. "Diego, I need you now."

I craved her as well. When I inched the tip in, she gasped and pulled back. "Condom?"

Ah, that human necessity. "I can't carry diseases or get you pregnant. But if you want, I'll wear one for you."

"Oh, right. Vampire perk?"

One of the few. "Yes. You okay then?"

She gave me a small smile. "Definitely." She guided me inside.

As I sank in, a rumble unfurled within my chest. "Fuck, you feel incredible, Nova."

"So good," she murmured with a low sigh.

I rocked into her over and over, deeper and harder each time. When I was on the cusp, I pulled back and slowed down. She climbed on top and straddled me, slowly rolling her hips as she glided up and down.

Sweet nirvana, it felt incredible. I gripped her sides as she rode me. As her pace quickened, she ground harder. I sensed she was on the edge. My fangs emerged, begging for a sweet taste. I tried to hide them so as not to frighten her.

It was too late.

She dropped her head back and cried out.

Damn, the sweet pulses and sound of her rapture were too much. I was right there with her.

"Do you want to bite me?" She asked in a velvety tone.

Damn, the sensuality in her question stoked an urgent pang of hunger. "Yesss," I admitted. Despite the terrible ache, I had to find some control. "Sorry, I know that scares you."

She ground down. "No, it excites me." She tipped her neck near my mouth. "Do it, Diego."

Raw need spiked and a feral growl ripped from my chest. Every part of me was already so on edge with potent lust. Her invitation was too much to resist. I flipped Nova onto her back, slipping out of her in the process. Eager to be inside her again, I drove in and covered her neck with kisses.

The call of the blood beneath her soft skin hummed, an irresistible song. My muscles tensed as I thundered in anticipation of this feed I'd so desperately wanted since I first inhaled Nova's scent.

I opened my mouth wider, bent down, and sank my fangs into her flesh. She cried out, but held on to me. As her delectable blood coated my tongue, sweet liquid fire shot through my veins.

Her moans softened with pleasure. I fed from her, ravenous for more of this unrivaled experience.

I couldn't hold back any longer. Pressure intensified as her blood filled me with new vigor, and I erupted with a thunderous climax.

NOVA

When I woke it was after ten in the morning. Diego slept soundly with one arm draped around me. I lingered for a few minutes, replaying the amazing night.

I slept with a vampire and let him bite me. And hell's bells, it was hotter than Hades.

Since I couldn't lie around in bed all day, and Diego would likely sleep for a while, I slipped out from under his arm. After I put on the blue dress, I tiptoed the walk of shame through the house to return to my aunt's apartment. No, my apartment. I had to start calling it that.

Why did I feel any shame? We were consenting adults. Still, I wasn't ready for Sebastian and Lucas to see me slipping out of Diego's room, knowing that I'd slept there, if they'd even made it home at all last night. I was supposed to pretend to be Diego's girlfriend, not actually have sex with him.

Today was November 1st. My rent was due on the first of the month. Ah, did that mean the guys would be paying me rent today? The idea of Diego slipping me a check after he slipped me something else last night made me squirm.

Oh well, what could I do? Wait, I should be thinking about what I had to do on my epic lists. Time to hit the trusty ol' planner so I could check things off with a sense of accomplishment—and maybe a shiny new sticker or two.

When I opened my planner, I read today's list, which included switching over bills to my name. Let the fun begin.

After I took a quick shower, washing myself with favorite rose water-scented body wash and shampoo, I pulled on a pair of black leggings and an oversized light blue shirt. When I checked my phone, I read a text from Gianna to let me know she'd gotten home fine. Nothing out of the ordinary happened at the club. It was a wild night with many celebrating Halloween in costume, but no trouble.

I sighed. That was a relief.

Who was the witch killed yesterday? I bit my lip. It was unlikely that I knew her since I knew few people in town. I called Colleen at the store, but it went right to voice mail. The store was closed today.

After a quick search online to try to find out anything about what happened with the murder, I found nothing. Before I fell too deep down a rabbit hole of unexplained murders thought to be related to the supernatural, I put my phone down and got to work. Today was paperwork day. I needed to go through what I could before the real estate agent came tomorrow.

A twinge of discomfort twisted inside me. The idea of selling this house and returning to New York didn't have the same appeal as it had when I'd first arrived. The longer I stayed in the house, and the more comfortable I became with practicing magic to clean and protect it, the greater my connection.

Also, there were the guys—especially Diego.

Stop it, I reprimanded myself. *You can't change your life because of one night of hot sex with a vampire. Come on, you're not that naïve.*

Right. I'd seen too many relationships fail to think that sex meant anything beyond several amazing orgasms.

But after lunch, Diego came over and helped me clean out some garbage from the basement.

After we were covered in dust, he flashed a devilish grin. "You know what this means?"

"What?"

"We should shower together."

I laughed. "Oh, is that right?"

"Yes. Saves on the water bill." He led me upstairs. We shed our clothing on the way to the bathroom in my unit, leaving a trail from the bedroom.

I ran my hands down his naked chest. "Thanks for looking out for me."

"I like looking at you, too." He trailed his fingers from my throat to breasts.

Once we were in the shower together, we kissed and caressed each other. Since he was a head taller than me, I arched onto my tiptoes and then placed one foot on the edge of the tub. He adjusted his stance, but with our height difference and the confined space, body parts did not align well. After more slippery, awkward attempts, Diego pulled back. "Shower sex is overrated."

"Agreed." I put my foot down.

Bedroom sex was not.

Once we were horizontal, and I had the comfort of soft bedding rather than hard cold tile pressed against me, our height difference no longer mattered.

DIEGO

I woke early in the afternoon. The sound of an unfamiliar female voice coming from downstairs captured my attention. Nova was talking to a woman.

When I'd come home from work before dawn, I thought about going to Nova's bedroom. We'd spent a great day together. Not only was the sex phenomenal, but we cuddled in bed and had watched Monty Python sketches for an hour until I had to go in to the lab. She was likely sound asleep, and I hadn't wanted to startle her yet again, so I'd gone to bed alone.

After I dressed, I stepped outside my bedroom and overheard the conversation. They were discussing the house and its condition.

Was this a real estate agent? It sounded like one. Why didn't Nova tell me one was coming? I descended the stairs. The woman had her graying hair pulled back into a little clip. She noted things on a clipboard.

Nova caught my questioning stare and then avoided eye contact. A shifty sign. "Oh, hey Diego."

The way she said it in that higher pitch edged my bullshit detector up another notch. Was she keeping something from me?

"Hey," I replied.

"This is Taryn," Nova added. "She's checking out the house."

Taryn extended her hand and greeted me. I shook her hand.

"It's a good house. Spacious." Taryn glanced around. "It just needs some updating."

"If I won't get in the way, I'll sit in the living room," I said.

"No, not at all," Taryn replied. "I'll finish up on the other side and be out of here shortly."

Nova gave me a sheepish look before leading Taryn through the kitchen into the other apartment and closing the door. I opened my laptop and pretended I was interested in what was on the screen. With my hearing, I caught bits of conversation, and it definitely sounded like Nova was looking into selling the house. That hit me like a punch to the gut.

Why hadn't she mentioned anything to me?

After about twenty minutes of dark speculating, Taryn said she'd be in touch and the door closed. I waited a few more minutes to see if Nova would come over to talk. Maybe explain the situation.

She didn't.

Had I been setting myself up as a fool to think that our time together meant anything to her other than a hot hookup while she was in town?

Closing my laptop, I placed it on the coffee table. I walked over and knocked on her door. "Nova, it's me."

She let me in. "Hey, Diego." Her shifting gaze belied her cheerful tone.

I stepped into the living room. Although I tried to restrain my troubled emotions, they seemed to simmer right beneath my skin, threatening to break through. "So you're going to sell the house?"

"Well, uh, I don't know. I'm looking into my options."

That made sense, but her evasiveness about it bothered me. "It's strange that you didn't mention it to me."

She hunched her shoulders and bit her lip. "I didn't want to, you know, upset you."

"Upset me?" I repeated and pointed to my chest. "Why would you think that?" Despite my attempt to sound neutral, I could hear the defensiveness in my tone. On one level, I knew it wasn't warranted. This was her house, and she could do whatever the hell she wanted with it. She was an adult, and she could sleep with me and leave, too.

But none of those rational explanations grabbed my common sense, not when her omission bothered me like a splinter beneath my skin.

"Sure, it would be common courtesy—especially since you started sleeping with one of the guys who live under this roof."

"Easy, Diego." She raised a hand. "Obviously, I need to find out the condition and the value of the house before I make any decisions." She gestured to me. "Who knows, maybe you guys will want to buy it, and everything will work out for all of us."

"Oh, is that how it is? Just wrap everything up and be done with it like that?" I brushed my palms together. Hearing the bitterness in my tone, I wished I could stop.

She frowned before staring at me with confusion. "What's going on? You know I'm only here to take care of my aunt's estate."

Only? That one word sealed it. "Oh, I see. You're *only* here to deal with the house. Which means I've *only* been a minor diversion from your weighty responsibilities of home ownership."

"What?" She blinked at me.

I was a fool to have any feelings for her when all she wanted was a little fling before she left. She'd soon be gone, just like everyone else.

Just like Diana.

Was I wrong to think they were different?

"I see how it is." I turned to walk back into my apartment.

"Diego, why are you being like this?" She caught up with me and touched my arm.

I spun toward her. Before I could hold it back, I barked, "I thought there was something developing between us, but I see I was wrong."

"Diego…" She sighed. "I don't know what to say. I've enjoyed all the time we spent together, but I don't want to complicate things. I'm already so confused about everything."

"I get it. This was just a hookup." I motioned between us.

"No, it's not like that."

"I need to get ready for work." That was a bullshit excuse since I wouldn't be going anywhere until sundown, but I had to get away from her. Before she could say anything else, I walked out and closed the door behind me.

CHAPTER 10

NOVA

Wow, I hadn't expected Diego to react like that yesterday and still didn't know what to make of it. I sorted through dusty books on the main floor, boxing those I would never read. It was good that he worked last night, as we could both use some space. I still wasn't ready to deal with what happened as I tried to sort through increasingly confusing feelings. From the first moment I'd met Diego, he'd been a conundrum, and every moment since grew more convoluted.

Yet, I couldn't deny I'd developed feelings for him. But what could that possibly mean in the scheme of things? It was definitely less complicated if we kept things casual.

I'd worked up the nerve to sleep in my aunt's bedroom again. Since I'd cleared the space of dark magic, I forced myself not to let myself get spooked. I mean, I was still blown away that I'd even managed to do *anything* with magic. It was strangely empowering.

Fortunately, it was an eventless night.

After breakfast, Gianna came over to help me pack some boxes and bring them to charity. I gave her a quick tour of my apartment and the shared kitchen. Fortunately, none of the guys were around—well, specifically, Diego. No need for the awkward morning after just yet.

When we returned to my living room, Gianna motioned around. “It’s such a great set up. There’s no way your apartment in New York is this spacious.”

“True,” I agreed. “But that doesn’t mean I’m going to move here.”

“So stubborn,” she said with a half-smile. “It’s astounding to me that you’d choose some crappy expensive shoebox that you share with others over this.”

“Don’t forget, I work at a publishing house in Manhattan,” I pointed out. “Which is pretty sweet.”

She tapped her fingers on her thigh. “And have you missed it at all?”

Gianna had me there. The truth was I hadn’t missed much—not my job or coworkers, apartment or roommates or the subway hustle to get to and from work each day. I didn’t miss the work since my supervisor asked me to pick up some projects this week.

“I can’t change everything and move here,” I replied.

“Why not?”

Good question. I exhaled with a huff. “I don’t know.” I raised my hand to my forehead and rubbed. “What do I have here besides a house?”

She placed her hand on her chest and arched one of her perfect brows. "Me."

"Yes, you," I agreed. "But it's not like we didn't talk while I was gone."

She rolled her eyes. "Talking on the phone isn't the same. It's much better when we get together like this." She tilted her head. "I miss having you here."

"I miss you, too," I admitted.

We tackled the numerous knick-knacks in the living room, from figurines to empty planter pots to candle holders.

"You sure you can't think of anyone who might want any of these?" I asked as I picked up a ceramic figurine of a woman.

"No. This stuff might have been sentimental to your aunt, but..." She shrugged.

Gianna was right. I didn't have any connection to any of these items, so they just looked like dust collectors.

"You might as well donate everything you don't want. Eventually, it will end up in the right hands."

I glanced around the room with all the books and plants and what nots. "That's going to be a lot of hands."

After we filled a box, Gianna clapped her hands on her thighs and flashed a mischievous grin. "So did you and vamp guy kiss and make up last night, preferably with some killer, hot make-up sex?"

Why did she have to put it that way? I'd given Gianna a quick summary yesterday. I blew a strand of hair out of my eyes. "Nope. I figure we could each use some space."

Gianna tilted her head and scrutinized me with a knowing gaze that called me out on my bullshit. "Is that what you want?"

I ignored her skepticism. "It's what's best," I dismissed. "We agreed it was just a fling. Now that we hooked up, it's out of our system, so we can put it behind us. Why make our lives any more complicated than it needs to be?" A part of me whispered *You're full of shit.*

When Gianna said, "You're full of shit," I gasped.

"Can you read minds now or something?" I asked. "Or have you always had that ability and you kept it from me?" I thought of all the embarrassing things I must have thought about as a teen in my angst-ridden, awkward, the-world-hates-me phase and cringed.

Gianna scrunched her nose. "No. It's written all over your face. You have this sappy, longing look like you want to go over there and ride him like you just got a cowgirl license."

My cheeks reddened, but I laughed. "Jeez Louise, I was *not* thinking that. And that doesn't even make sense."

"Yeah, sure." Her words dripped with sarcasm as thick as Vermont maple syrup.

My tongue seemed thicker, and I swallowed. Maybe she was a tiny, itty-bitty, miniscule bit correct.

After we filled a few more boxes, we brought them to a charity drop-off site and then stopped for a bite to eat downtown. A woman walking toward us from the opposite direction on the sidewalk looked familiar, but I couldn't place her.

"Sadie!" Gianna declared.

Ah right, Sadie—the sadist with the laser. No, I shouldn't think that. She was sweet. I was just a wimp.

After they greeted each other, Sadie appeared to recognize me, but in an odd manner. She turned pale and stared. "I'm so glad to see you're okay, Nova."

What a perplexing reaction. "I know I was a pain in the ass at the appointment, but I wasn't *that* bad, was I?"

"It's not that." Sadie exhaled. "I was worried and thinking of reaching out. Because remember what you told me about the night terrors or whatever that was?"

How could I forget? "Yes."

"And I'd mentioned how my friend experienced the same thing?"

With a wary nod, I replied, "I remember."

She pressed her fingertips together and then tapped her mouth. After she lowered her hands to her sides, she said, "Here's the thing. My friend died suddenly on Halloween."

"Oh, I'm so sorry," I said.

Sadie leaned forward and whispered, "Traces of dark magic were found."

My heart leaped against my ribs. The three of us exchanged glances that all but screamed in the silence. What the hell was going on in this town?

GIANNA TRIED to calm my anxieties after we saw Sadie yesterday, yet the tension remained.

When I'd called Colleen to report it, she replied, "Yes, we're aware. She's the young woman I mentioned."

I explained the darkness I'd encountered in my aunt's bedroom, and how Sadie had mentioned her friend had experienced something similar. "Is there anything I should do?"

"Not that I can think of," she replied. "Just be vigilant. If you notice anything odd, call me."

I tried to put it out of my mind as I worked on the house. Sebastian and Lucas had helped me clear out some boxes from the garage.

"So, uh, Diana really did a number on Diego." I attempted to sound nonchalant, but wasn't sure I sold it.

"Uh huh," Lucas said as he taped a box. "Bloodsucking leech."

"She wrecked him good," Sebastian agreed. "But he's a good guy."

"He sure is. Shadow loves him because Diego spoils him with affection." Lucas laughed. "But not as much as I do."

"Don't let Diego's gruff exterior fool you," Sebastian added.

"I won't." With a smile, I said, "Although it was quite a rough introduction, he's been nothing but considerate ever since."

"Oh, good," Sebastian noted with approval. "I can't believe how he acted that day."

"Don't worry. It's been much better since. Maybe he's more comfortable around me."

"He seems to be in a good mood since the ball, Nova," Sebastian pointed out as he carried a box. "Whatever you did with helping him face Diana the night of the ball must have helped him with a breakthrough of sorts."

Although I wished that to be true, I didn't want to reveal exactly what we'd done that night. The horizontal tango and blood drinking could remain Diego and my secret for now.

When we were done in the garage, Lucas took some of my aunt's plants and brought them to his apartment.

"You sure about this?" he said. "I don't mind coming over and taking care of them."

"They'd be happier with you," I replied. "You've been taking good care of them."

After lunch, I went up to my attic room where my aunt had created her workspace. It was the most perplexing task yet. What on earth should I do with all these jars of herbs and oils and all kinds of weird things that my aunt used in her spells and potions? I figured once I got a handle on everything there, I could sort it into piles to figure out how to donate them.

Trunks were stuffed with old clothing. Boxes housed old papers. Other containers were full of mason jars, some empty and others full of contents I wasn't sure I wanted to identify.

As I rifled through the contents as careful as possible, I choked on dust. Although her altar was spotless, the boxes shoved against the wall gathered a fine coating of old attic ambiance complete with the smell of soot.

After I pulled yet another box away from the wall, a straight crack in the panel behind it struck me as odd. It was perfectly straight within a seam, but then ended a foot or so from the floor. I pushed on it, and the wall pushed in.

My eyes bulged. It was a door. My fingers trembled as I opened it. Inside was a white plastic box. Curious.

My heartbeat quickened. I pulled the container out. When the label read ornaments, excitement vanished like a popped balloon. Why would my aunt hide ornaments back here? If I had a secret nook like this, I'd use it for something more valuable than ornaments. It would probably go into the donate stash. I opened up the lid. What was inside was definitely *not* ornaments.

It was a book. It appeared ancient and bound in brown leather. A pentacle was carved into the cover, as was an eye. Bright gems in the color of ruby, emerald, amethyst, and sapphire were attached to the four corners.

I put my hand inside the box to take it out, but paused with my hands hovering. The oddest sense of change swept through me. By opening this book, it might lead to a new chapter in my life. Literally. Some stories could change you forever.

I swallowed, took a shaky breath, and lifted the book. It was heavier than I thought, and the leather was soft against my fingers. I held the weight and stared at the cover for a solid minute before I worked up the nerve to open it. When I did, a piece of parchment fluttered out. "Dear, Nova" was written at the top.

A letter addressed to me in a mysterious old book hidden in the wall? What the what?

I ran my hand over my temple with my free hand. Why would my aunt take these odd measures? I blinked through the haze of questions. Did she sense I'd find the letter one day, even here?

But what if I never took the time to look that closely in the attic? None of it made sense.

Stop asking questions and read the damn letter.

After a shaky breath, I did.

. . .

Dear Nova,

If you are reading this letter, then you have found our family's Book of Shadows. And that means the magic is still in you. Only a witch with powerful intuition would be able to find it.

My heart thudded. What magic? I'd just been sorting through boxes. I continued to read, hoping she'd explain it.

Now that this heirloom is in your hands, you must take great care to protect it. It contains powerful spells collected by our family over centuries.

You may be wondering why I am leaving this in your care and why I left the house to you as well.

Well, yeah. That was only the tip of the mountain of questions.

If you're reading this letter, I most likely have moved on. And that means significant changes for you, beyond inheriting my property.

When you were a young girl, it was clear to see that you'd be a gifted witch. You could sense things others couldn't. You could move objects without touching them. You were a natural at working with the elements and were fascinated with fire. The things you could do would frighten your parents, especially your father. He didn't trust it.

I don't know if you remember the accident with fire.

. . .

I WISH I DIDN'T. Unfortunately, the worst memories tend to be the ones that stick, at least in fragments. It's like walking into a fly trap. It's almost impossible to pull off the damn strip, and once you do, the sticky residue lingers.

NOBODY KNOWS what you were trying to do, but whatever spell you called was powerful enough to generate fire. Unfortunately, it grew beyond your control. Your mother ran into your bedroom and rescued you just before the smoke would have smothered you both.

After the incident, your mother and I argued. Your parents wanted nothing to do with magic from that point on. They thought it was too dangerous. It had almost killed you.

I recognized what you had done as a sign of much magical talent. After all, fire is an element. Water is another, which can douse the flames. With the proper training, you could grow into a gifted witch who could help others, like many of your ancestors before you. Your parents disagreed. They thought I was trying to exploit you.

That was never the case. I always had your best interests in mind. You're my niece, and I love you. But I don't fault them for thinking that way. I'm not a parent, and I can't imagine the instinct one feels to protect their child.

Your mother and I quarreled for weeks. She begged me to put a block on your magic to prevent you from using it. Eventually, I relented. Almost immediately afterward, I regretted it. We had a huge fight, and she ordered me to stay away from you. That's why I was no longer part of your life. It wasn't that I didn't want to be. I did. I got updates from friends over the years, but stayed away as your mother requested.

I don't want you to blame your mother because every parent does what they think is best for their child, and she did it to protect you. But on my death, the block will break. You're an adult. The choices you make from this point on will be yours and yours alone. You can choose to go on living the life you've had, which I'm very proud of. You were always such a voracious reader as a child, and I love how you've chosen to help other children discover a world of books.

But there's another way as well. In this book, you'll discover keys to help you develop your magic. And what you do with that is up to you.

Whatever you choose, be wary. Many who have craved power have searched for it throughout the centuries. You must keep this book from getting into the wrong hands.

If you do not want to follow this path, contact the Salem Supernatural Network. They will make arrangements to make sure it remains protected.

Blessed be,

Aunt Margaret

After I finished the letter, my mouth was open wide enough to catch a spider. I shut it and pressed my hand to my lips, feeling them tremble. So much unidentified emotion hurled through me.

I stood and paced in the round tower room, occasionally darting glances at the leather book. Wicked bats and flying monkeys, how could I process what I just read? I'd once been able to move things with my mind—that wasn't possible.

Was it?

Raising my hands, I stared at them like they were foreign objects. She'd said when she died that the block on my magic would be lifted. I traced back to the day of her death. That was the day I'd felt that weird jolt on the train.

Had that been the moment that my magic returned to me?

Several minutes later, I gazed out the window as I paced in circles around the perimeter of the room. I still couldn't believe what I read. The information flowed into and over me, threatening to drown me in its depth.

How could I parse through what I'd learned? What I'd been entrusted to protect?

I thought of my parents. The knee-jerk reaction was to lash out at them and ask *whhhyyyyy*?

But I understood what my aunt had explained. I'm sure saving your child from a fire would be traumatic and lead to taking drastic measures to avoid it ever happening again. But to make a huge decision like that *for* me? That was taking it too far.

Once I became an adult, I should have been able to make my own decision regarding magic. Maybe I was reacting like a sullen teenager, but that's how I felt—like a part of me had been taken away. Because it had been.

I glanced at the book. Just opening it had changed my life drastically with that one letter. What else was inside?

Carrying the book over to a lavender arm chair, I sat with it on my lap and flipped through pages of old parchment with varied handwriting. Some pages listed the names of women who had contributed to the book, dating back to England in the 1600s.

The book also included the phases of the moon, different moons during the seasons, and the types of magic most optimal during those periods. A listing of festivals and traditions followed. After that was a collection of spells and the ingredients necessary. Several witches listed their preferred methods on setting their altars, grounding themselves, calling the elements, and casting circles. What followed were instructions for clearing one's mind as well as a number of spells and potions, such as those for protection. I snorted.

That would have come in handy recently.

The spells were written by various witches in my family over the decades. The earlier ones appeared to be in Latin, but the more recent ones were in English. The language didn't appear to be what mattered, but the intention behind what was chanted. Anyone could say words, right? They could say things like I love you, but if they didn't mean it, they were merely words.

But when they were true, those three words were truly magical.

Ah, what did I know?

I'd dated, but never experienced a relationship that intense—definitely not the kind that Diego had with agreeing to become a vampire for love. I placed my hand on my heart. That was morbidly romantic.

I continued flipping through the pages. In the latter half of the book, a page noted a warning:

The pages beyond this point involve complicated magic and should not be practiced as trivial?

I hesitated, the incident with the fire stoking fear like rising flames. After several shallow breaths, curiosity propelled me forward. The pages contained instructions for dealing with matters I thought fictional, such as banishing evil spirits, demons, and so on. Damn…

Mouth agape, I closed the book and stared out the window. What should I do with this powerful Book of Shadows I didn't know existed until minutes ago?

My aunt had noted the responsibility to keep it out of the wrong hands. The most obvious choice would be to return it to where it had been hidden for now. The only ones who would be able to access it were the guys, but since it had been stowed here for some time, I figured it was safe.

After I stashed the book and returned boxes to hide the secret wall panel, I returned to pacing. I needed to talk to someone about this, but who? Who could I trust with the life changing discovery?

I thought about talking to Diego, but we hadn't known each other for long. Besides, with how weird we'd left things the other day, it would be strange to confide in him—not to mention how I'd be telling a vampire about a powerful witch's grimoire in a house he inhabited. In my limited knowledge of the supernatural world and this book, that could be a big no-no.

I'd known Gianna since childhood and trusted her with my life. I called her. When she answered, the sound of a Motley Crue song played muffled in the background.

"Are you at the club?" I asked her.

"Yes, what's up?"

"Are you busy?"

"I can talk for a minute. Let me step outside. It's so loud in here." While the music faded, she said, "I was just talking about you."

"To whom?"

"This hot guy who came in tonight. Tall, dark, and handsome with black hair you want to run your fingers through and green eyes that are so vivid you'd want to drown in."

My nostrils flared. That didn't sound enticing.

"There's something about him that's hard to describe," Gianna added. "Yummy, though. A body any red-blooded female would want to roll with. I think you should meet him."

I swallowed. "Gianna, you know I have something going on with Diego."

"I thought that was just a fling, and it's done," she replied with confusion.

I resisted a groan. That had been precisely what I'd told her, but like she'd pointed out, I might be full of shit.

"Well, I told him to sign up for speed dating and that you'd be there. He seemed interested."

"Oh, jeez." I exhaled. Perhaps Gianna wasn't the right person to call since she was already trying to set me up with someone else. "Why aren't you going for him then?" I asked.

"Because I'm a good friend," she replied. "And I think a little bit of this Dr. Feelgood is exactly what you could use right now."

Some friends suggested ice cream. Others offered wine. My half-siren friend considered a hot hook up as medicine for any ailment.

"Gianna, I discovered something strange in my aunt's attic just now."

"What?"

After taking a moment to try to sort through all I'd learned and the order in which to present them, I decided that chronological was best. "While clearing out her things, I found a book." I didn't mention where I was or where I'd found it as the responsibility to keep it guarded had already been pressed onto me. "Inside it was a letter addressed to me." The contents of the letter tumbled out in a rush of word vomit as I tried to hold myself together.

"Oh, honey," she said. "I'm so sorry. I understand why you're upset."

I had managed to hold the tears back, well, most of them. "And now I have this book I'm supposed to take care of. How would I, out of anyone, know what to do with it?"

"A family Book of Shadows?" She groaned. "That does sound like an epic ton of responsibility."

"Exactly. And since I didn't know I had the ability to do any sort of magic until a short while ago, I feel the least capable of protecting it."

"Hold on a sec." It seemed more like twenty before Gianna said, "Okay, I'm back. Funny, it was the hot guy I was just telling you about. He came out for a smoke. I walked away so he won't overhear me."

Shit, maybe I shouldn't have been telling Gianna any of this. And perhaps not over the phone. It could be tapped.

Ugh, I dropped my head back. Now what—I was getting paranoid? All because of this stupid book.

"What are you gonna do?" Gianna asked.

I rubbed my eyes. "Good question. I don't know where to start. I need to talk to my mother, first of all."

"Good plan. Talk to your mom and let this all sit before you make any rash decisions." A man's voice called Gianna from the background. “Shit, I need to get back inside. Want to come by for a drink?”

“No. I think I need to let this settle. My mind hasn’t just been blown, it’s like someone lit fireworks off for the grand finale inside my brain.”

“Totally get it. How about I come by tomorrow morning?”

“That would be awesome, thanks.”

“Listen,” she added. “I know you’re freaking out, but look at the bright side. You always thought you sucked at magic, but that’s not the case. You might find this new world one you flourish in. Maybe you should follow along with what’s in the book and learn more about what you’re capable of.”

I grunted. “That’s probably not a good idea. After all, I just inherited a house. I don’t want to accidentally set it on fire.”

CHAPTER 11

DIEGO

After dark on Tuesday, I headed into work. I hadn't seen Nova since my outburst yesterday and still wasn't sure what had come over me.

While I ran blood tests, I replayed our conversation again, the same as I'd been doing for the last day. Had I overreacted?

Probably.

Did I *have* to come off as a defensive jerk?

Nope.

If I couldn't handle a fling without getting butt-hurt over her living her life, it was probably better that I stayed away. Since she was leaving by the end of the week, it would've ended soon enough, anyway.

It didn't make it any easier to forget her.

How could I? Not only had we had fun together, but the sex had been amazing. Just thinking about how good it had felt to drive inside and taste her blood got me semi-erect.

Maybe I was giving up on this too easy. Sure, Nova would be returning to New York soon, but it wasn't a planet away. If we wanted to keep this thing going on, we could visit each other. Weekend trips wouldn't be difficult to arrange. People did it all the time.

When I returned to the house before dawn, I added some pouches of blood to the fridge. That was one of the benefits of this job—the blood I was given. It reduced my need to access it in other ways, such as taking it from a human donor. Although after I'd had a taste of Nova's blood, how could I not crave it?

I glanced at the door leading into her apartment. Was she upstairs in bed sleeping? A yearning rose to go to her, to wake her up with kisses all down her body. I'd make her cry out in pleasure before I entered her silky-soft body and then sink my fangs into her delicious veins. I walked over and placed my hand on her door.

Walk away. Walk away now.

Forcing my fists to my side, I stopped myself from acting on that plan. After the way I acted, would she want anything to do with me anymore? I doubted it. Besides, why would she get involved with a vampire when she could have any guy she wanted? I'd been fooled by a vampire. I wouldn't want Nova to get involved with one—even if it was me.

She deserved better.

. . .

WHEN I WOKE the next morning, Nova remained at the forefront of my mind. I went downstairs to get a pouch of blood. Sebastian stood statue still in the kitchen, nostrils flared.

"What's up with you, man?"

He snapped out of whatever daze he was in. "It's this scent. Someone must have been here lately. It's been driving me crazy."

Who had been there as of late? "The real estate agent came by on Monday."

Sebastian nodded, but didn't seem convinced. "Maybe that's it."

"Are you all right?" I asked. "You seem off."

He rolled his head from left to right, making a cracking sound. "I'm fine. It's just… unfamiliar." That distant expression remained on his face. "I need to get ready to go into the restaurant."

After he ran up the stairs two-at-a-time, I entered the kitchen. My gaze traveled to Nova's door. I opened the fridge and downed one of the pouches of cold blood to try to drive away the hunger to go to her.

A few minutes passed with me pacing through the living room, wrestling with what to do. Unable to take it any longer, I strode back through the kitchen and raised my hand to knock on the door. When I heard her speaking to someone on the phone, I stopped. The conversation sounded tense.

Scolding myself not to eavesdrop, I forced myself to walk away.

NOVA

The conversation wasn't going well.

After a restless night trying to sort through all the info, I'd Face-timed my mother. True to form, she made it all about her from the start.

"I've been meaning to call you, Nova," she said. "We've been so busy. You know how things get down here."

Sure. She didn't have a job, let alone two. What did she know about being busy? Getting her hair and nails done for the next golf event?

Biting that statement back, I chose to focus on the reason for my call. "Yes, Mom."

"Where are you? It doesn't look like your apartment."

"I'm in Aunt Margaret's house." *My house, my house.* Would I ever get around to thinking of it as mine?

My mom wrinkled her nose. "Oh. I should have recognized the *decor.*"

"Yes, Mom, you should. After all she was your sister."

"Have you gotten the house on the market yet?"

"No. I never said that it was definite. And that's not why I called," I snapped in frustration.

"Why did you call?" My mom asked.

I took a deep breath and rubbed my forehead. I couldn't see this conversation going anywhere without escalating tension.

"Aunt Margaret left me a letter."

My mom's face dropped. "Oh, did she?" Although she attempted for a neutral mask, the false lilt gave her anxiety away.

"Yes. It explained a lot." I pinned my gaze on her.

Her bottom lip trembled. Fear flashed vivid in her eyes. For a second, I felt badly for being the cause of it, until I remembered she'd been keeping something from me for all these years.

Averting her gaze, she twisted a lock of hair around her finger. "About what?" The fake disinterest in her tone didn't fool me.

"Why I haven't been able to use magic since I was a kid," I replied.

She froze, and for a moment, I wondered if it was the screen.

When she moved her mouth again, she said, "I wouldn't believe anything she had to say."

"It did seem to make a lot of sense, but I don't see why she would have any reason to lie to me."

"About. About what?" My mom blinked a few times.

"Mom, enough," I barked. "You know. You insisted she put a block on my magic. Yes, I get that you were scared and trying to protect me, but you also kept it from me all this time."

"I did it to protect you." The neutral mask fell, replaced by anxiety. "Do you know how terrifying that fire was? You almost died!"

"I get that, Mom. Trust me. I've been looping through this all night. What bothers me is that you kept this ruse going. I'm an adult now. Don't you think you could have told me at some point, instead of letting me think I was unskilled this entire time? A failure?"

A tear ran down my mother's cheek, smearing her mascara. "You're not a mother. You don't know what it's like. I'd do anything to keep you safe. Anything. Even if it means you hate me."

"I don't hate you," I said. This was the problem with talking with her. She'd somehow turn this around and make herself the victim, so I'd end up apologizing to her. Not this time. "I don't want to argue about this. I just wanted to let you know. The block was lifted when Aunt Margaret died, which means—I can use magic again."

"Oh Nova, don't," she begged, eyes stark wide with terror. "The fire…"

"I'm not a kid anymore, Mom. I've already cleared the dark magic I found, which may have killed Aunt Margaret."

"What?" If her eyes bulged any wider, they'd pop from her skull. "Nova, don't you see how dangerous it is being there, just like I feared? You need to get out of there at once."

"I can't. Not while I'm figuring things out. And don't worry, I put new protection spells on the house."

She blinked at me as if trying to translate a foreign language. "I know you're upset with me, and maybe you have every right to be. But please, promise me one thing."

"What?"

"Be careful. I beg you not to mess with magic. Promise me that you won't do anything else."

I stared into her distressed eyes and felt her pain gnaw at me, but I wouldn't let it hold me back this time. Not anymore. "I can't promise that."

I RESUMED the task tackling house cleanup to keep my mind off my conversation with my mother. Once I returned to the work-space in the attic, curiosity compelled me to open the Book of Shadows. I scoured through the pages, fascinated. Now that the block was lifted, could I pull off any of these spells?

After the call with my mother, even considering doing so made me feel like a rebel. Was there any taste more tempting than forbidden fruit?

As I flipped through the pages of the moon phases and the best times to perform certain types of magic, I decided to try some. After a lifetime of guilt, I was sick of being afraid of magic. It was my damn house now, and if I burned it down, so be it.

A flicker of guilt followed. Hopefully, that wouldn't happen because I kind of liked my roommates, especially Diego. Since I'd already managed some basic clearing and protecting spells without blowing anything up, I figured it was safe.

Raising my aunt's wand, I tried a few levitation spells using the Latin word, "*Ortum*."

To my shock, an orange and yellow maple leaf floated up from the altar. Maybe Colleen was right when she'd said she sensed magic in me.

When my stomach growled, I looked at the time. It was already two in the afternoon. Gianna was supposed to have stopped by earlier. I texted her to see if she still planned to come over and headed out to grab a sandwich. An hour passed, and she still hadn't replied, so I called her. It went straight to voicemail. I left a message asking her to call me.

By seven, I was worried. I called the club. "Hi, is Gianna there?"

"Not yet," a woman replied.

"Is she scheduled to be there tonight?"

"Who's calling?"

"Her friend, Nova. Is this Kylie? We met the other night."

"Oh, yeah. Hey Nova. She was supposed to be here an hour ago. She should be in soon."

"Okay. Please have her call me."

I bit my lip and tried not to fret. She was likely caught up with a guy and having a grand ol' time.

Right, tomorrow she'd tell me she got tied up and then with a laugh, would add "literally."

I spent the rest of the day consumed by the book and practicing spells. Shadow the cat came to watch, curling up on a windowsill. By the time I went to bed, I'd managed to cleanse my aura (if it worked), remove any traces of the block on my magic (if any remained), and worked with the element of air to make a leaf levitate. What a day. Magic was far more exciting than packing up dusty boxes.

When tomorrow came and I still hadn't heard from Gianna, dread twisted inside me like coiled snakes. Something was wrong. Was my friend in trouble?

CHAPTER 12

DIEGO

Nova entered the kitchen, her face pale. "Hey, Diego," she said with what sounded like forced normalcy.

Although things were still awkward between us, my concern for her pushed that away. "Is something wrong?"

She exhaled. "It's my friend, Gianna. She was supposed to come by here yesterday." Her lips formed a grim line and shook her head. "She didn't. She also didn't show up to work last night. I just went over to her place to see if she's there and no luck." Raising her gaze to meet mine, she said, "I'm worried about her."

"Come sit," I insisted and patted the spot beside me on the couch. Once she did, her scent washed over me. Tension ebbed from my taut muscles. How could she have such a soothing effect on me?

Nova summarized the events of the past day or so of searching for Gianna. "I called Colleen, the witch who warned us the night of the ball. She noted that they'd look out for her. She mentioned that another witch had gone missing. Since Gianna isn't a witch, she told me to try not to worry. But how can I not?"

"I understand." Now I was the one concerned. With another witch missing, what did that mean for Nova? "You need to be careful as well," I noted. "Considering what's going on."

She rubbed between her brows. "I know. But I also can't just sit around here and not do anything without knowing if Gianna is okay."

I placed my hand on hers, aching to be able to take away her distress. "What can I do to help?"

"I don't know." She dropped her head back. "I don't even know what *I* can do to help." She glanced to the front door. "I was thinking about going to her club to see if I can find out anything there, but Colleen told me not to go out alone."

"You won't." I stood. "I'll go with you.

Nova stood and gazed at me with wonder. "You will? Aren't you working tonight?"

"I can go in later." As long as I was done before sunlight, I'd be fine. I glanced at the door. "Come on, let's go."

THE DANGER ZONE had a dark vibe and decent music, much better than those college bars with shitty pop that I wouldn't be caught dead in. My nostrils flared. Technically, I was dead in this one and any location I stepped in. The curse of the vampire.

The Rolling Stones' "Sympathy for the Devil" surrounded us as we walked over to the bar. The bartender had blue hair divided into two braids.

"Hi Kylie, it's me, Nova. Gianna's friend. I called earlier. This is my friend, Diego."

I nodded and said hello. Kylie responded with a half smile.

"Did she ever come in?" Nova asked.

"Not yet." Kylie picked up a white cloth and wiped down the bar.

"Shit." Nova exhaled. "Did you see her talk to anyone the last time she was in?"

"Yeah." Kylie shrugged. "Of course. She talks to a lot of people."

"Anyone stand out?" I asked.

Kylie hmmed and tapped her fingers. "There was a guy she sat with at the bar for a bit. Killer hot."

"What did he look like?" Nova asked.

"Dark hair. Bright green eyes. Nice body."

Nova turned to me. "She mentioned talking to a guy who looked like that." Facing Kylie again, she asked, "Did she leave with him?"

"Not that I saw." Kylie shrugged. "But who knows? It gets busy here at night."

"Did you catch his name or anything else?" I asked. Who did I think I was—Sherlock freakin' Holmes?

"No."

I asked whatever questions that came to mind that might give us any clues. The sooner we found Gianna, the quicker Nova would stop worrying.

What was going on with me lately? Why did I care so much? How had Nova become such a part of my life in such a short time? I wanted to care for, protect, and make her happy.

Kylie stared at us both as if assessing what she should tell us. "I don't think he was—" she bent down and whispered, "human." She gestured to me. "Like you, but different."

She must have sensed I was a vampire. "What do you mean exactly?"

"I've worked here long enough to differentiate humans from supes. It was in his intense eyes. And the way he moved. More graceful than humans. Like a suave, almost floating sort of gait."

Nova glanced around. "And you haven't seen him since?"

"Nope."

"When you see Gianna, please tell her to call me." She grabbed a drink menu. "I'm going to hang out a bit and wait."

Kylie said, "I wouldn't worry about Gianna. She can take care of herself. Besides, she likes to have fun. I'm sure she found someone she likes, and she's having a good time right about now."

"I hope you're right." The worry in Nova's tone indicated she didn't appear as convinced.

Maybe I could help ease her concerns.

After Kylie moved down the bar to take another order, Nova said, "It's just hard to shake off this sense that something's wrong."

"I know just the thing to help take off the edge," I said. "Let's start with a drink."

I leaned closer to look at the menu with her. My nostrils flared. "You smell good."

Nova smiled. "Thanks. That's a compliment coming from a vampire, I'm sure."

"You bet it is." I pressed closer to her to glance at the menu. "Let me take a look." The drink options were printed in a black bifold menu that had the dungeons logo embedded in the front cover. Inside were a variety of cocktails with cheeky twists on rock and metal songs. The "Rock You like a Hurricane" looked like a recipe for regret the morning after, judging by the amount of alcohol. Nova chose a "Love is a Battlefield" cocktail which had a mix of vodka and cranberry juice.

I ordered a glass of red wine. When I placed the order, Kylie winked. "Got you covered with the house special."

After she returned with our drinks, I knew why. The wine had blood in it.

"Nice," I told Nova. "They have options for the bloodthirsty."

"Oh, are you thirsty?" Nova asked with a hint of suggestiveness.

A craving stirred in my veins, and my fangs itched for a taste of her. "I am indeed."

Our gazes locked, and I had to swallow. Nova did something to me that knocked me off-kilter. This beautiful witch enchanted me.

When her phone vibrated, Nova broke eye contact and answered it. Less than a minute passed before she ended the call.

"That was Colleen. A detective from the Network is going to come here to talk to us." Nova smoothed out her outfit and glanced at the door. "Let's grab a booth."

Ah, we were back to business. The spell was broken, and with it, so was the fantasy of taking Nova home with me tonight.

NOVA

Zoe, the detective from the Salem Supernatural Network stood at barely five feet tall. When I glanced at the slight points to her ears that poked through her red hair, I guessed why.

"You can see them?" she asked.

Shit, I'd been caught staring. "Ah, sorry."

"No reason to be. Just wondering since most can't. Elves disguise our ears with magic so we look more human."

I was keenly aware of Diego's quiet presence beside me. His thighs and upper body touched mine. I found it soothing, protective—and something more. But now wasn't the time to think of anything sensual, so I shoved the awareness aside.

"Tell me about your friend," Zoe said.

I repeated what I'd told Diego earlier and added, "Gianna mentioned this guy she was talking to. She was trying to get me to meet up with him at a speed dating event here tomorrow."

Diego stiffened at my side. Although I felt guilty for bringing it up after what had gone on between us, I thought it important to tell the detective. "He was one of the last people seen talking to her."

He'd also overheard her talking to me about my family's book. I hadn't told Diego yet, and I kept it mum now. Since I was tasked to protect this book, I shouldn't go around announcing its existence.

"What do you know about him?" Zoe asked.

I shook my head. “Not much. She mentioned him having dark hair and green eyes.” Avoiding Diego’s probing stare, I added, “And a good body.”

“Sounds like he’s the only lead we have at the moment,” Zoe said. “I’ll see if I can get a list of who registered and come tomorrow to question him.”

“I should come, too,” I piped up.

“What?” Diego asked.

The surprised glance on Zoe’s face mirrored his.

“Because he might talk to me. After all, Gianna mentioned me being in town and attending the event.” I turned to Diego. “Not that I’d agreed to sign up.” Turning back to Zoe, I added, “It’s the least I can do to help find her.”

“Whoa.” Diego raised his hands. “That sounds like a terrible idea. You’re putting yourself out there as bait.”

“Right,” Zoe said. “Not only have witches been killed, but we’ve been chasing crimes throughout the city.”

“I think that’s even more of a reason for me to get involved to help save Gianna,” I said.

Zoe studied me. “With Gianna not being a witch, it’s probably unrelated, but I suppose it doesn’t hurt to see if you can find anything out.” She tipped her head. “If he shows up.”

“It could be dangerous,” Diego protested.

I motioned through the club. “I wouldn’t be alone. I’d be in a club full of people.”

“But none of them would be looking out for you in case something goes wrong,” Diego added.

That was true, but I was used to that being the case.

Diego shook his head. "I can't let you take this on yourself."

"What?" I stared at him in surprise.

"I'll come with you," he declared. "To make sure you get home safely."

"Brilliant." Zoe said. "You can keep me abreast of the situation. If this guy shows up, text me." She glanced at her phone and frowned. "I've got to go." She stood. With her short stature, it didn't give her much more height from when she was sitting. "We'll talk tomorrow."

After Zoe left, I said, "I should sign up for the event." With a groan I added, "If Gianna hasn't done so already." With a guilty grin, I added, "Diego, I was not planning to attend."

He rolled his shoulder, avoiding eye contact. "Why not? You're free to do what you want."

True. We had no obligations or commitments to each other. "Okay. I'll sign up."

When I went to talk to the bartender, Rula, she looked into the registration on a laptop. "You're already on the list."

Ooh, if I could access the names, maybe I could send it to Zoe since she'd dashed out before talking to anyone. "Can I see who else is registered?"

Rula's lips tightened. "No."

I bit my lip. How could I get her to reveal the info to me? "I need it to help Gianna out." Technically, that was true."

"No can do." Rula wiped some glass rings from the bar. "I'm not sharing it unless I hear it from the boss herself."

Ugh. Gianna couldn't provide that info if she was in trouble. I stifled a groan. "Can I have the details about tomorrow then?"

Rula narrowed her gaze. "You should have received a confirmation email."

I prickled under her scrutiny. Jeez, I was trying to help out her boss. "Gianna signed me up." I shrugged. "Maybe she used her email and meant to forward it to me."

After sizing me up some more, Rula forwarded the email to me. Geez, she was tough. But at least I walked away with more info to carry out the plan.

As I made lunch the next day, the guys were in the living room. Diego filled him in on the plan and then asked me what time the event started that night.

I opened the email with the registration info. "Eight." While scanning through the details, my gaze stopped on something. "Oh, wait, that won't work."

"What won't?" he asked.

"You watching out for me. The club is closed to the public during the event. Only those who are registered will be allowed in."

"Even better." Sebastian clapped Diego on his back and smiled. "Diego will need to register."

"No way." Diego shook his head. "I don't need to do that."

"You have to," Sebastian protested. "How else are you going to watch out for Nova?"

"I can stay on watch outside," Diego replied. "You know I hate those kind of forced conversations."

"Terrible idea," Lucas countered. "What if she gets in trouble *inside* the club?"

"You need to sign up." Sebastian raised a hand palms-up. "Besides, it will be good for you. "

Diego replied with a doubtful grunt.

"How so?" I asked.

"He can get out and meet people." He faced Diego. "While you're being all brave looking out for Nova and helping find her friend, you might even meet someone special."

Diego and I exchanged a glance and then quickly broke eye contact.

"Wait a minute." Sebastian stared from one of us to the other. "Is something going on here?"

"Oh shit, yeah." Lucas rubbed his hands together and leaned forward.

"I don't know what you're talking about," Diego dismissed.

"Then meeting new women will be good for you," Sebastian replied with a knowing grin.

Lucas's mouth curled up with mischievous satisfaction. With the way that Sebastian and Lucas stared at Diego and then me, it was clear they suspected something going on between us—and it amused the shit out of them both.

CHAPTER 13

NOVA

Diego and I had decided to enter the club at different times the next evening, so it didn't look like we were together. I walked in first, to the sound of Fiona Apple's "Criminal" playing, which didn't help with how sneaky I felt going about this stunt. Round black tables were set around the club with framed numbers. I fought the urge to leave. This strange, rushed way of meeting people was not for me. I preferred a slower introduction rather than getting thrown into a situation of meeting several men in one night. Would I even remember their names or any details about them?

It didn't matter. I was here to help find clues about what happened to Gianna.

Right. I did not have to look at this as an attempt at an awkward precursor to dating. This was a mission to find answers, not a potential partner.

Glancing around for a guy who might fit the description of who she'd spoken to, I came up short. Oh well, it was still early.

After I stepped up to the registration table, a woman gave me a name tag and a list of tables for my schedule that evening.

"Got it." I attached the name tag and headed to the bar to get a drink. Tonight definitely required some liquid courage. I ordered a Blue Monday and sipped it as I meandered.

When Diego entered the room, I couldn't help but stare. Rather than his usual dark colors, he wore a lighter gray sweater that fit him well, showing off his lean torso. I wasn't the only one who noticed him. I crossed my arms and clenched my teeth. On realizing how jealous I was reacting to the other women scoping him out, I forced my arms back to my side.

Diego caught my gaze, and my mouth felt dry. Heat rose in my cheeks. What was it about this vampire that stirred such a potent reaction in me? Wild vibrations simmered beneath my skin, heating me up with a warm and pleasant tingle.

Time to focus on the task. I glanced at my card. My first round was at table three, a meaningful number for a witch.

The host introduced himself as Michael. He had a winning smile and surfer-blond floppy hair.

"Welcome to Danger Zone. I hope you're as excited about tonight as I am."

Some of the attendees cheered or raised their drink.

"All right. At the start of the next song, you're going to go to the first table noted on your card. After two songs play, you'll hear the bell. That means it's time to move on to the next one. After four rounds, we'll have a short break. Then we'll have the next four."

Eight rounds or sixteen songs. That shouldn't be too grueling.

"At the end of the night, make sure you note who you'd like to meet up with again on your card before you drop it in the box at the registration table. Tomorrow, you'll receive an email with matchups, and you can contact one another if you'd like.

As 3 Doors Down's "Kryptonite" began, Michael announced, "It's time to head to your first table."

I took a hearty sip of my cocktail and headed to table three where I sat opposite Gerald. He had sandy-brown hair and hazel eyes. He was pleasant enough. When he learned I lived in New York, we spent much of the time discussing what we'd seen on Broadway. I didn't feel any spark, but it wasn't a bad conversation at all. More like someone you might chat with at a party to avoid standing in awkward silence. When the second song ended, we wished each other a good night and moved on.

That wasn't so awful. At my next table, I met Angus, a burly guy with a full beard who I guessed might be a shifter. The way he looked me up and down left little to the imagination of what he was interested in.

No, thank you.

The next two table mates weren't as blatant. Steve worked in a music store by day and played guitar in a band on weekends. Roger wore black-framed glasses and worked in a college library. Once again, no sparks with these two, but the conversations weren't awful.

Michael took the microphone again. "Congratulations, you made it through the halfway point. Since nobody has left in tears or vomited in their lap, I'd say we're off to a good start."

During the break, I headed into the restroom. When I returned, Diego sat at the bar with a beer in front of him.

I walked over to him. "Hey, stranger. How's it going so far?"

Diego growled. "Painful." He drank some beer.

"That bad, huh?"

He turned to face me. "Yeah. This whole event seems so unnatural to me."

Diego was enduring this painful situation to help me. "Thanks for coming tonight. I know you did so to look out for me." I touched his arm.

He glanced down at where my fingers remained on and then returned to meet my eyes. "No problem."

The intensity in his blue gaze pulled me in. I pulled my hand away. Why did I have to touch him and make things weird? Although it might have meant nothing with anyone else, even a small gesture like that with Diego struck me as intimate.

He glanced around the club. "Any sign of the guy?"

I shook my head. "No."

He grunted. "Maybe it's a dud."

My stomach sank. He could be right, in which case, this was a stupid plan.

"Drink?" he asked.

"Sure. The Blue Monday was good."

He ordered it and handed the blue cocktail to me. "Good luck."

"Thanks." I took a sip of the fruity beverage. The sweetness hit my tongue before the alcohol aftertaste. "I'll meet you out front when it's over."

"I'll leave first and wait for you out there. Don't go anywhere without me." If his words alone didn't convey the intensity of the situation, the grave stare sealed it.

DIEGO

The announcer said some more stupid shit before the next song played and he told us to start the second half of the night. This was excruciating. I should've known that I couldn't pull off this role. I'd never even been in a school play.

When I sat down at the next assigned table, I exhaled. Here we went again with me faking interest in the conversation.

The pretty brunette with a heart-shaped face sitting across from me chirped on about her job right away. "I love working on people's hair. When they come in looking like a plain Jane, and I transform them with a great haircut and an eye-catching color, it's the best feeling."

"Oh, yeah." I attempted to sound interested, but my tone sounded disingenuous.

She didn't seem to notice as she continued to talk about herself. I nodded or made sounds of acknowledgment to make it appear that I was listening, but probably didn't sell it well, especially as I kept stealing glances at Nova.

I told myself it was because I was here to protect her, but the jealous pangs indicated there was more to it. I was not comfortable with this. Seeing her sit with other men who tried to impress her struck me with a hot stab in the gut. I hated thinking she might enjoy herself. Who was to say she wouldn't be attracted to one of the guys and hit it off?

She had every right to do so. I had no claims on her, nor she on me.

On the next round, I tried to contribute more to the conversation. A tall, slender vampire sat across from me with silvery-blonde hair and green eyes. She'd turned many heads tonight. I would have likely been one of them had I not been so interested in what was going on with Nova. She sat across from a tall guy with hair as black as his jacket. I couldn't see his face, but saw hers, and when it appeared to light up, it felt like I'd been staked.

The vamp said, "Looks like you already found who you want tonight."

"What?" I pulled my gaze back to her.

"You're staring at that woman."

I adjusted in my chair and drummed my fingers on my lap. "It's not like that."

She arched her brows. "Yeah, sure."

I asked a couple of questions to get her to talk about herself, but once again found my interest wandering over to Nova.

The vamp stood. "This isn't going to work. Have a good night."

Great, I was doing such a bang-up job at acting that I couldn't even keep a woman sitting across for me for two songs. The truth was I wanted to get out of there. So far, the night had provided no insight other than how I'd rather be at home with Nova than anywhere else.

She glanced at me from the opposite end of the room and tilted her eyes as if to ask what happened. I shrugged, like it was no big deal and then sipped my beer. She returned her attention to the person sitting across from her. Now that I didn't have anyone to entertain with a half-hearted attempt at conversation, I could watch to see what was going on there.

Nova lowered her hand to the side of the table and then pointed at the man opposite her. She moved her hand back and forth pointing at him.

It had to be the guy. I pulled out my phone and texted Zoe.

She replied during the next song. *In the middle of something. Will get there as soon as I can.*

NOVA

I found him. Inside I was doing a happy dance. This ridiculously hot guy with a strong jaw and piercing eyes had to be the one Gianna had spoken about. Diego didn't look half as thrilled as I pointed him out. In fact, he was brooding at the bar. The woman who he'd been sitting with stood near a wall, focused on her phone. Guess they didn't hit it off.

While a-ha's "Take on Me" played, I learned that Andre, the guy I was there to find, was new in town.

"How did you find out about this club?"

He rubbed his nose. "Word of mouth, I believe."

"Ah." From whom? "My friend convinced me to sign up. She owns the club. Her name is Gianna." I scanned him for any reaction.

Aside from a minor twitch in his jaw, nothing. Maybe I was barking up the wrong tree. I wasn't any sort of sleuth, but figured if he'd met Gianna, he might show some sign of recognition. Oh well, might as well keep him talking to see if I could get any more information from him.

"Do you live nearby?" I asked in a casual tone.

"For the moment."

That didn't reveal much, so I prodded, "So you're not planning on being around for long?"

He fixed his gaze on me. "I don't usually stay in any one place for long."

Hmm, then why would he be at date night? Oh duh, just to hook up.

"Does that mean you're looking to make new—um—friends?" Ugh, why did I ask it like that? It sounded naïve.

"Yes." He leaned back in his chair and flashed a decadent grin that I supposed was aimed to melt my panties off. "I would love to get friendly with you." He reached across the table and stroked my hand.

Ick. Although I wanted to yank my hand back, I forced myself to play along. If I wasn't able to get anything useful from this conversation, I could at least try to keep him interested in talking until Zoe came. Hopefully, Diego had understood my message and had texted her.

"I'd like that," I lied.

"Perfect." The smile morphed into a satisfied smirk. How did someone so attractive suddenly turn so unappealing?

I swore I could feel Diego's burning stare.

Andre leaned forward. "I'd like to learn more about you."

Ah, that was to be expected. I didn't want to tell him too much, but had to keep the conversation going. I tilted my head and flashed what I hoped was a flirtatious smile. "Oh, really? What would you like to know?"

He stared at me for a few seconds, gaze raking down to my breasts before rising back to my face. "You mentioned that you're new in town, as well. What brings you here?"

The muscles in my legs tensed. "Family."

"Family?" he repeated in a way that prodded for more.

"Yes." I brushed a strand of hair behind my ear and stole a quick glance at Diego.

He appeared to be paying close attention to me as he nursed a beer.

"Are you staying with relatives?" Andre asked.

"Sort of." Wariness crept up my spine. I wouldn't tell him where I was staying.

We tiptoed around with more small talk until he said, "A witch returns to Salem."

I leaned back in shock. "Why would you say that?"

"I can sense what you are." He brought his fingertips together and rested them on the table. "What kind of magic do you prefer?"

"What?" I shook my head. What an odd question.

"There are many types of magic. Do you focus on any in particular?"

"Uh… um." He threw me off guard with that question, and I had no clue how to answer.

"Certainly, you must gravitate to one in your family's grimoire?"

I gaped and then blinked. Why would he say that? I thought I was the one trying to get information, but sensed I was under interrogation. And he focused right on the book.

Scrambling to climb out of this hole, I turned the questions back to him. "Do you practice magic?"

He gave me a sage nod. "Yes."

"And do you prefer a certain type?"

His green eyes brightened with a flash of intensity. "I'm comfortable with all forms on the spectrum. So many witches shy from dark magic as if it's something to fear. It's part of the universe. After all, you can't have light without the dark."

A chill curled around my spine. That sounded ominous as fuck. Fortunately, the song ended, and I had my escape. "Nice to meet you, Andre." I forced a smile.

"A pleasure." He stood and tipped his head. "I hope we become *—friends*."

Yuck, yuck, yuck. No, way.

In the short break before the final speed date of the night, I headed into the ladies' room and splashed some water on my face. Andre rattled me, and I wasn't exactly sure why.

When I moved to my last table, Diego sat across from me.

I exhaled, relieved I wouldn't have to fake interest for two more songs. "I thought you were done for the night."

"I was until I saw that I'd matched up with you."

"Oh, I'm flattered," I said with a grin. I turned to see where Andre sat, but he was walking out of the club. "Shit. Please tell me you texted Zoe."

"Yes, she said she'd get here as soon as she could."

"Damn, he's leaving. He's the guy." I pointed to the door and stood. "Although he didn't reveal anything about Gianna, something is definitely off with him."

Diego rose. "Where are you going?"

"We can't let him leave." As I rushed to the club's exit, Diego walked with me.

"You can't go after him," he said. "It's too dangerous."

"Cover me then," I said. "But make sure you aren't seen."

Without waiting for an answer, I headed outside. Where the hell did Andre go?

Ah, near the corner of the black brick building, he held a lighter to a cigarette.

"Hey." I sauntered up to him. "You're not leaving already, are you?"

He lowered his hand and raked a bold gaze over me with a slow perusal. I resisted the urge to cross my arms over my breasts.

"I was planning on it," he said. "But now that I see you again, Nova, that's changed. I'd love to talk some more."

"Sure, I'd like that," I said. Motioning back toward the club, I suggested, "How about we go back inside for a drink?"

He wrinkled his nose. "It's too stuffy in there." He tipped his head in the opposite direction. "Let's walk along the shore."

Oh, hell. I didn't want to go anywhere alone with him, but also didn't want him to leave. As long as Diego covered me, he could text our whereabouts to Zoe. All I had to do was walk and talk. I'd try to keep the pace slow.

I forced a smile. "I'd like that."

CHAPTER 14

DIEGO

Why the hell did I agree to this? Not that Nova had given me much of a choice before she took off to carry out this insane plan.

As I followed, holding back in the shadows so as not to be detected, one thought repeated in my head like a drumbeat—this was a bad idea.

We'd gone completely off plan. And where the hell was Zoe?

It was too dangerous for her to go anywhere with this guy. Witches had been killed. Nova was a witch. We didn't know if he had anything to do with Gianna's disappearance, but this route was too risky.

As they approached the waterfront, a sense of dread rose as thick as the salty scent of ocean and seaweed. I had to stop this.

Jogging up to her, I interrupted their conversation. "Hey Nova."

She turned and blinked at me. “Diego?”

“Yeah. I was looking for you at the club. Someone mentioned you’d headed this way.”

She stared at me as if trying to read a secret language on my forehead. “Here I am.”

“I see that.” With a nod back toward the club, I said, “We need to talk.”

The dark-haired, too handsome guy stepped up. “We were busy. She’ll talk to you later.”

Nova bristled.

“She is quite capable of deciding for herself.” I stepped up to the guy. Who the hell did he think he was to try and intimidate me? His scent reached my nose. I couldn’t identify it, but didn’t think it was human.

“Actually, I better go and talk to my brother.” Nova slipped between us and gently pushed me back.

Brother? Whatever. As long as I got her away from him.

We walked away in silence. As we approached the club, Nova turned to me. “Did something come up?”

I clenched my jaw. “Yes. I couldn’t let you go off with him. What if he’s responsible for what’s been going on?”

Nova groaned. “That’s what I was trying to find out—and I was making progress by getting him to talk.” She placed her hands on her hips. “So you’re saying the only reason you pulled me away was because you were worried?”

I shifted my stance. “Technically, yes,” I admitted.

She tipped her head back and exhaled with frustration. "Diego, you shouldn't have done that."

"Why not?" I countered. "You going off with him wasn't part of the plan."

She brought her hands together and wriggled her fingers. "He was leaving, and Zoe hadn't arrived, so the plan changed."

"No. I couldn't let you do that. You're not trained to handle the situation."

She dropped her hands to the sides and her eyes widened. "Oh, so you're saying I couldn't handle it? I'm not smart enough to help my friend?"

I jerked back. "That's not what I said at all."

Nova's face turned red. "I'm sick of people making decisions for me."

"What?" Why was she getting all indignant over this?

"You didn't trust me to be capable of carrying this out. Just like my parents." She threw one hand up and dropped it to her side.

"Nova, what's going on?"

"Everybody thinks I'm some big fuckup who's gonna burn the house down and kill everyone in it."

What was she talking about? I blinked at her and slowly raised a hand. "Are you all right?"

"No, far from it. This is bullshit."

She turned and walked away.

After gaping at her retreating back and wondering what the fuck I'd said to set her off like a firework, sense returned to me. I ran up to her. "Where are you going?"

"I don't know."

"You can't be out here alone. Not with what's been going on."

She released an exasperated sigh. "Yeah, I'll get myself killed."

"Possibly."

"Screw this. I'm an adult. From now on, I decide what's best for me." She continued walking.

"That's fine." I kept up with her. "I'm not trying to make any decisions for you. But I'm also not going anywhere until I know you're safe."

She grunted, but didn't try to stop me. We didn't say a word on the way home. Once we arrived, she entered her side of the apartment without turning to me. After the door closed with force behind her, I stared at it.

What the hell was that about?

All I'd done tonight was try to look out for her. From forcing myself to endure the forced conversations during the speed dating and then through that painful silence as we returned here. If she couldn't appreciate what I'd done and wanted to freak out on me instead, to hell with her.

It proved that I was better off without her. Why deal with all this drama when I could avoid it? I could go back to simply existing and not feeling for anything or anyone.

It was safer that way.

NOVA

The next day I avoided Diego.

It was easy to bury myself with activity. Not only did I have cleanup tasks and calls for what I needed to get done around the house, but I had to work remotely on some projects that my boss asked me to take care of. It wasn't easy to forget about last night. I was still fuming about it, sick of people deciding what was best for me. Why couldn't Diego have trusted me and followed my lead?

Zoe called around ten in the morning, apologizing for not getting to the club in time.

"More craziness going on?" I asked.

"Like you wouldn't believe." She snorted. "It's like we have pranksters setting up magical mishaps throughout the region. As soon as we put out one fire—sometimes literally—something else comes up."

It sounded intense. At least, she hadn't mentioned another murder. I passed on the little information I knew, and she said she'd get his address from his registration form.

Not that my hunch seemed to be leading anywhere. When I'd brought up Gianna, he hadn't admitted to knowing her. There was that glint of something in his eyes, but it had disappeared so quickly, I might have just imagined it out of wanting so badly to find her. In which case, I'd be wasting the Network's time when they had so much going on.

Her voice lowered in warning, "You really shouldn't go anywhere alone until we figure out who's behind this."

That was what Diego had been trying to do and was the entire reason he suffered through the event last night. Shame rose like steam from a boiling kettle, and my cheeks warmed as I remembered my outburst.

Perhaps I'd overreacted a tad. I didn't need a shrink to figure out why. The discovery about what my parents had kept from me was still fresh. Diego had unfortunately been in range when I was frustrated, and I'd lashed out at him.

Maybe I should go over and apologize. I'd have to think that through since whatever was going on between us seemed to be more than a simple hookup. Was that even possible since I'd be leaving soon?

Not likely.

What I should be doing was getting my shit together rather than dealing with complicated boy stuff. Ugh, why were relationships always complicated?

At lunchtime, I peered into the living room. No signs of anyone. I made myself a peanut butter and banana sandwich and checked my email. Andre and I had matched. Ding, ding, ding!

Wait, was this good or bad? I didn't want to date him, yet couldn't shake the sense that he might know more than he let on. We chatted in short messages. He wrote that he'd like to see me again. We exchanged numbers.

I texted the update and number to Zoe.

Got it, she replied.

When I returned to my apartment, I wasn't up to dealing with house stuff just yet. Curiosity about my aunt's magic lured me up to her workspace.

I pulled out the secret book from its hiding space in the wall and sat in the lavender armchair. Over the next several hours, I practiced working with the elements, especially focused on spells for defense and protection—something I hadn't needed until recently. It was good to have them in my arsenal considering the situation with witches in the area. I learned how to call on the wind to block magical attacks like a shield and how to create a protective bubble around a small area.

When I learned to generate the tiniest ball of flame in my hand, barely larger than the tip of a match, I danced around with glee. I'd created fire and hadn't set the house ablaze. Progress!

After dousing the flames with a water spell, I moved on. That thrill of success led me to attempt more advanced spells, many of those involving magical combat. Bouncing around like a fencer, I blocked imaginary attacks and countered them both with and without the wand. What seemed to matter was not the words or the objects, but the intention behind them.

Not all of my endeavors were successful. When I attempted one type of block using a combination of earth and wind energy, the force knocked me on my ass. Literally. And then some. The movement was so powerful that my legs went up and over me.

Whoa, I definitely did not mean to do that.

Brushing myself off, I stood up. Fortunately, no one was around to witness my blunder.

The rebellious streak had taken hold, though, making me determined to master it. I continued to practice, and my ass kissed the floor a few more times. Eventually, I nailed it.

Zoe texted me back. *He used a fake name and address. We'll keep digging. Don't go meet him.*

I groaned. I should have known better. My stomach growled. When I glanced outside the window, the sun was setting. I'd completely lost track of time. I ordered takeout from a nearby sub shop and gobbled down a large chicken parm sub. My small successes with magic led me to return to practice instead of packing—one was definitely more satisfying than the other.

Exhausted, I took a small nap on the sofa. The phone woke me some time later. Expending all that energy must have knocked me out. The caller ID displayed Andre's name. Hmm, I didn't expect to hear from him so soon.

I pulled myself up to sit. "Hi, Andre. How are you doing?"

"Bring me the book if you want to see your friend again."

I blinked and then widened my eyes. "What?"

"I know you have a Book of Shadows, and I want it. Gianna is with me. Say hello to Nova."

"Nova, I'm so sorry," Gianna said. "He overheard me talking to you and—"

"Enough," Andre hissed. "Nova, you know I have her, and you know what I want."

I gasped. "Don't hurt her!" I stood and paced in an erratic stretch through the living room.

"That's up to you," Andre said.

"Why do you want it?"

"Not your concern."

I disagreed since it was a family heirloom.

"Come to Salem Willows now," he demanded. "If you tell or bring anyone with you, it's over. Your friend dies. And then you're next."

He hung up, and I stared at the phone, my hand trembling. My mind buzzed with frantic ideas on what to do. A clipped call changed everything in a flash.

Focus. I had to be sensible. Gianna was in danger. What the hell could I do to help her?

I groaned. Andre had made that clear enough to be seen on a flashing billboard in Times Square. The question was should I listen or try something else?

I could tell the Network. Maybe they could stake him out.

No, it was too dangerous. If he knew they were there, he'd kill Gianna. Could I tell my roommates? They were supes. They could help, right?

Too much was at stake with Gianna's life. I couldn't tell anyone. Not even Diego.

My forehead was so hot, covered in perspiration. I wiped at it while I told myself to *think, think, think.*

My gaze drifted to the Book of Shadows. My aunt had entrusted me with this and within days, I'd failed. All because I'd freaked out on discovering the letter and called Gianna.

Shit, this was all my fault.

Was there anything else I could do? Any other option?

Nothing came to me.

I had no choice but to do what he demanded. But I wouldn't go without any protection. What could I use to help me?

I zipped up to my aunt's workspace and scoured the space. Too bad I hadn't been able to have more time practicing on how to defend against a psychopath who'd kidnapped my best friend to get his slippery hands on my family's book. I grabbed my aunt's wand from her altar and shoved it into my coat pocket. Perhaps it was futile, but better than nothing.

With a heavy cloak of failure on my shoulders, I picked up the book to deliver it to Andre.

DIEGO

Since I'd woken up I looped through all that had happened last night with Nova. Why had she freaked out like that?

Sure, I understood on some level. She thought she was doing what was best to find her friend, but it was too dangerous. Witches were being killed, and she was a witch. Going with some mysterious guy wasn't a risk she should have taken. Although I spotted her, anything could have happened, maybe even so fast that my vampire speed wouldn't have been enough.

I was better off without her in my life anyway. It was easier to live cut off from the world because that way nobody got hurt.

When I'd gone down to the kitchen to retrieve a blood pouch. Nova's scent was fresh. It had drifted to me, and I'd moaned with euphoria.

I'd debated going to talk to her. Things had gotten heated out of fear and frustration.

No, it had just been her scent affecting me again. I'd stepped back, forcing myself to clear my head.

After I'd drunk a pouch, I'd gone into the basement. If I couldn't get her out of my head, I'd beat it out on the drums. I'd played for a solid hour until my arms hurt and sweat rolled down.

I'd headed upstairs to shower and then had read in my room before heading to work. I hadn't had much to do at the lab, so it was a short shift.

When I returned home, Nova's car was there. I glanced at her apartment and forced myself to ignore the ache to go to her. Instead, I went straight to my room and tried to read my book.

Minutes later, a car started outside. I rushed to the window. It was Nova. She was leaving. Alone.

Shit. She shouldn't be going anywhere by herself. All the reasons I told myself why I'd be better off without her vanished. Instincts propelled me to sprint down the stairs and out the front door. I made it outside just as she pulled away.

Dammit, now what? I could jump in my car and follow her. That wouldn't go over well, not after last night.

Yet, the alternative would be worse if she was killed.

Screw it. I had to follow her and see if she was okay. Even if she cursed me through the end of my immortal life.

CHAPTER 15

DIEGO

I jumped into my car and sped to catch up to Nova. "Come on, come on," I declared to the person in front of me as I banged my hand on the steering wheel.

I shouldn't have brooded all day. After we'd cooled off, I should have gone over to her place and done something to make her laugh. Maybe toss her the killer bunny stuffed animal.

I snorted. Wow, what a genius I was—did I really think throwing a stuffed animal covered in fake blood at her would be something she'd think was funny? No, more likely she'd think I was some deranged stalker.

Even my attempt at humor to lighten things up had a dark side.

Finally, I passed the driver. Once I caught up to Nova's car, I slowed down. She couldn't know I was following her. It would make the situation between us so much worse.

While I trailed her, I remained as far back as possible. The traffic was sparse this late at night. She headed down to Salem Willows and pulled over. I turned my lights off before I parked. She scanned the area. Fortunately, I'd turned the lights off just in time, or she would have spotted me.

She held something in her hands. Even with my vampire sight, I couldn't make out what it was. Then she headed into the park. Why would she do that? Was she out of her mind?

I had to go after her. Aiming for stealth as I slipped into the park, I felt like some creepy prowler. The moon shone down through the branches of the trees, which loomed like dangling arms ready to reach out and grab me. I didn't like this situation, not one bit.

Although I couldn't see Nova, her scent remained. It was fresh. Up ahead, footsteps crunched over twigs and fallen leaves. That was the problem with walking here. I stepped on grass as much as possible to silence my approach.

The muffled sound of voices rose. It was Nova and a man.

Shit.

Who the hell would she meet out here?

I had a sinking feeling I knew who it was, and hoped like hell I was wrong.

NOVA

My hands were clammy. I did not want to walk into the darkness alone. But if Gianna was in there, I had to do it.

Forcing one foot in front of the other, my heart galloped as I stepped in between the willow trees. My breath came in pants, the wisps were visible before me in the cool night.

When I spotted Gianna, I rushed forward. That asshole Andre had tied her to the trunk of a tree.

“Gianna!” I called out. “Are you okay?

“Don’t do it, Nova,” she implored. “Don’t give him anything.”

“Quiet,” Andre barked and pointed at her.

She snapped her head back and her eyes widened, but she didn’t say a word.

“What did you do to her?” I demanded.

“You brought the book,” he replied, ignoring my question. “Smart choice.” He reached out. “Hand it over.”

“Untie her first.”

He walked over to Gianna and yanked on the rope. She cried out.

“Leave her alone!” I shouted.

He sneered. “She’ll be back with you in seconds if you do what I say.”

What could I do? I couldn’t leave her like this. “Who are you really? I know you used a fake name and address. What do you want?”

He sneered. “What everyone wants. Power.”

I shook my head. “That’s not true.” I cocked my head. “Why are you killing witches?”

That was a baseless bluff on my part as I had nothing solid to connect him with the murders.

He leaned forward in a mock bow. "There's nothing greater than taking magic from the source." He inhaled and tipped his head back. "Delicious."

"You sick fuck." I stepped backward. "Did you kill my aunt?"

He scowled. "That damn witch escaped before I could steal all her magic, but it was too late for her. The darkness was already taking hold." His mouth curled into a victorious leer.

"You bastard." I stepped forward ready to push him, but he raised a hand and it stopped me from approaching.

It prevented me from moving, period. My muscles froze, the same way it had in my aunt's bedroom. Darkness seemed to slither around my ankles. My breath came quicker, and my skin prickled with cold goosebumps.

Was that what had happened to my aunt? He'd attacked her with some sort of spell, but she'd managed to get away. Once back in the safety of her house, the dark magic must have finished her.

What might happen to me next. Fear clutched my throat, and I swallowed.

A breaking twig nearby sounded as loud as a boom in the otherwise silent night.

"Who the fuck is there?" Andre gestured with a circular motion. "Illuminate!"

I was able turn over my shoulder. With Andre's attention diverted, whatever he'd used no longer imprisoned me.

"Diego." He appeared under a muted glow like a spotlight shone through the trees.. Diego's eyes were as wide as twin moons in a starless night.

Andre seethed. "You knew the conditions about bringing anyone." When I turned to him, he had his arm raised as if preparing to throw something at me.

Diego hollered, "No!" and rushed forward, tackling Andre in a movement almost too quick for my eyes.

A blast of electric blue light erupted from Andre's fingertips, sizzling against a tree. Wood cracked overhead and I jumped to the side before a heavy branch crashed where I'd been standing. I dropped the book and stared at that branch. It could have killed me.

Diego had just saved my life. My breath came quick and hard as I gaped at him, now grappling on the ground with Andre, slipping over each other on the fallen leaves. What the hell could I do? I pulled out the wand and searched my brain for what I'd been practicing in my aunt's workspace, but my mind turned as blank as an empty journal on January first.

When they broke apart, a malevolent smile spread across Andre's face. He raised his hand and chanted something that sounded Latin.

Shit. I couldn't let him hurt Diego.

"Don't!" Raising the wand, I summoned the elements using a jumble of words from spells I'd practiced earlier.

For several heartbeats, nothing happened. Of course not. I'd just mumbled nonsense. I might as well have sang the wrong lyrics to a rock song—one of Gianna's specialties.

Andre wasn't moving. He appeared to be frozen as still as stone.

A swirl of cold wind rushed with an iridescent mist. It surrounded him. Diego stepped back and stood beside me.

Gianna gasped. "What's happening?"

Fuck if I knew. I rushed over to her and untied her with fumbling fingers.

"Are you okay?" I asked.

She glanced down at her restrained body. "Yes, I think so."

Once she was free, she hugged me. We then turned to Andre.

He burst through the haze with an explosion of vapor that rained over us. Diego stepped before us, spreading his arms as if trying to shield us. We ducked and covered our heads. When the cascade of air caressed our skin, it was cool, not harmful.

Andre roared and raised his hand at the three of us huddled together. Blue electric lightning fired from his fingertips.

"No." I raised my hand and pictured a shield. The blue bolts appeared to hit something and then stopped.

Andre's eyes widened as he stared at me. He lowered his hand and his face contorted with anger. He powered toward me, raising his arm again as if preparing to clench my throat.

This time I was ready. I opened my palm and chanted, *Wind and fire, take him higher.*

A gust of wind swooped in and circled around Andre, capturing him in a funnel. The swirl of vapors rose, and as they did, their color intensified. Pale colors darkened to fiery red, orange, yellow, and blue. He bellowed and rage contorted his features, but the winds stifled the sound. He struggled to get out of the tornado rising around him, but it lifted him off the ground.

"Whoa," Diego uttered, hushed amazement in his tone.

"What in the world did you do?" Gianna asked.

I couldn't reply, fascinated by what unfolded with Andre. Plus, what could I say?

Finally, part of one of the spells I'd practiced came to me—one to banish evil.

I gathered energy from deep inside myself before I projected it forward, using the wand as a focal point. "*Relinquo*!"

The funneling mist appeared to slow and harden around Andre. As it did, the fiery colors faded.

And so did he.

His body appeared to lose substance as he turned translucent, mirroring the vapor surrounding him, which now looked more like ice.

The ice splintered, forming cracks. His mouth opened as a howl came out, but it was cut short as his body froze and faded.

"It's only just begun." His voice was little more than a hoarse whisper.

Andre and his magical prison shattered with the sound of breaking glass.

I ducked. Diego jumped on top of me and Gianna, shielding as much of our bodies as he could with his. The surrounding air seemed palpable with energy before it exploded, and thousands of tiny fragments rained down. The freezing pebbles pummeled us.

Countless seconds passed before the explosion was over. I peeked out from under my hands. Frigid fog hovered as if we were in a steam room.

"Are you okay?" Diego pulled himself to stand and helped us up.

I blinked and then scanned myself. Aside from a few scrapes on my hands, everything appeared to be intact. My jeans and jacket provided some coverage. "Yeah, you guys?" I stared at them both.

"Fine," Diego replied, despite the cuts on his face. At least, they appeared superficial.

"Think so," Gianna said. She appeared dazed, but as flawless as always.

"Is he gone?" I asked, not sure I could believe it.

"Looks like it." Diego nodded with approval, and then a glimmer of wonder flashed in his eyes. "You did good, Nova. Real good."

I threw my arms around him. "I'm so glad you're here."

He gave me a one-sided grin. "Good. I thought you might chew my head off for following you."

"And saving my life?" I shook my head. "I don't think so." I cocked my head. "Why did you follow me?"

He squared his shoulders and then nodded. "I saw you leaving, and I wanted to make sure you were okay. By the time I ran outside, you'd pulled away, so I jumped in my car."

I kissed him on the cheek. "I didn't have a choice. He told me he had Gianna, and he'd hurt her if I told anyone. Trust me, if there was anyone I wanted by my side, it was you."

We stared into each other's eyes with a silent understanding between us.

Remembering Gianna was there, I turned to her. "Are you sure you're okay?"

"I'm fine." Her expression turned troubled. "I'm so sorry, this whole thing was my fault."

"What? How?" I asked.

"That demon overheard me talking to you. He wanted to get the book, but couldn't get into your house as it was protected. So he used me as bait to get to you."

I flushed. "Andre was a demon?"

She tipped her head. "That's what he claimed. He said he wanted the book to be able to use witch's magic and overthrow them. He wanted to take control of Salem."

Holy bats. How close we'd gotten to that happening. Not only had witches been killed, but he almost had a book that would give him more power.

"What did he mean about it only just beginning?" I asked her. "Are there others?"

She bit her lip. "I don't know. He locked me in a room and only revealed so much to me."

My gut sank as I realized my culpability in her imprisonment. "I'm the one who should be apologizing to you." I pointed to my chest. "I called you and told you about the book. If I hadn't opened my big mouth and blabbed, you wouldn't have been caught in my mess. I'm so incredibly sorry, Gianna." My bottom lip trembled.

She gave me a warm smile. "It's not your fault at all. That's what friends do—we confide in each other."

I hugged her once more, longer this time. Her familiar vanilla shampoo scent wafted around me, a comforting sign that she was okay. I couldn't imagine a life without her. The past couple of weeks reminded me of how close we were and how much I missed her. I didn't have any relationships a fraction like this with anyone in New York.

Gianna pulled away and ran one hand through her dark hair. "Once I've slept for a thousand hours and my brain finally catches up to all the craziness, let's have a big, fat cocktail. Or four."

"That sounds like a splendid idea." I glanced at Diego and grinned. "I guess this is a good time for introductions."

After we took care of the pleasantries, Gianna said, "Thanks for coming, Diego."

Diego shrugged in acknowledgment. "I barely did anything. It was all Nova." He turned to me. "How did you learn to do that kind of magic?"

I picked up the book and held it close to my chest. "I kind of winged it from my family's Book of Shadows."

"I didn't know there was one," he replied.

"We have a lot to catch up on, Diego. I found a letter in here that um..." After shifting uncomfortably from one foot to another, I said, "It might have contributed to my outburst yesterday when you were only trying to help me. I'm sorry."

He cocked his head. "Why don't we go back home, and you can tell me everything there?"

Home. That had such a comforting ring to it, especially with Diego there.

I smiled at him. "Sounds perfect."

Gianna stepped closer. "Can I get a ride home, Nova? I just want to be in my own bed and not move until I have to."

"Of course," I agreed. "Let me call Zoe first and let her know what happened here."

I pulled out my phone and called. She picked up right away.

After I told her a condensed version, she said, "You winged a spell and banished a demon?"

"He claimed to be a demon, and he's gone. So maybe?" An unfamiliar sense of accomplishment filled me.

"Impressive." Her voice had a tinge of awe. "I'll come and investigate."

While we waited for Zoe, I filled Diego in on the letter and the book.

He pulled me into an embrace. "No wonder you were on edge."

Relieved he could forgive my outburst, I wrapped my arms around him tightly. When Zoe arrived, she paced over the grounds where we'd last seen Andre. "Smells like vile ass demon, all right." She stopped and stared at me. "That's quite some magic you performed, Nova."

"I wish I knew what I did. My mind went blank, and I just blurted out different parts of spells."

"Sounds like you relied on intuition rather than memorization."

I turned my hands palm up. "Possibly. I just couldn't let anything happen to Diego and wanted to protect him."

"Yes, that makes sense that you drew on your deepest feelings. Intuition is often powerful and effective when it comes to magic." She cocked her head as she steadied her gaze on me. "We could use you at the Network." She raised a finger and added, "Especially if what the demon claimed is true, and the danger isn't over. With all the chaos we've been chasing and trying to control lately, it's highly possible he had help. But I'd never trust anything a demon claimed. They're full of lies. Even so, you should remain wary." She nodded to herself. "We are short-staffed and could definitely use a witch like you."

I blinked at her. My aunt had mentioned how the book could change my life, and she wasn't kidding. Even my half-assed, clumsy attempts at magic had led to a job offer. "I don't know how to respond."

"Think about it," she said. "Don't worry, we provide training. You wouldn't be thrown out to face things on your own." She tipped her head. "Although you did pretty damn good yourself."

Her praise moved me, almost to tears. "Thanks. I'll think about it."

"I'm going to stay here and continue investigating."

Diego, Gianna, and I walked out of the park back to my car. I turned to him. "I'll see you back at the house."

He raised his chin. "I'll follow you."

"Diego, you don't need to do that," I replied. "The danger is gone."

"We don't know that for sure, so just humor me, okay?" He rubbed the back of his neck. "It's been a crazy night, and I'd go mad with worry about you getting home safe."

"Okay," I agreed. After all, I'd been quite acquainted with worry over Gianna and was sure it etched a worry line as deep as the Mariana trench between my eyes.

I kissed his cheek before I climbed into the orange Mini, and Gianna sat beside me. When I turned the car on, The Cure's "Friday I'm in Love" played on the radio. I smiled, remembering how Diego and I had planned to tell his ex that we'd met at a Cure concert.

Was that some sort of sign? Did I even believe in that?

Big question. I hadn't believe a lot of things until I'd returned to Salem. For one, that I ever thought I could do a basic spell, let alone conjure enough magic within to overpower a demon. And two, that I could ever feel a sense of belonging in a town where I'd considered myself an outcast. With Gianna, the guys, and most of all, Diego, it started to feel more like home.

As soon as we pulled away from the curb, Gianna tapped her thigh. "So that's the vampire you've been hooking up with?"

I sighed. "After all that happened, I'm hoping it's more than just a hook up."

"Ah, you care for him. I can hear it in your voice."

"I do," I admitted.

"Good. He seems like a good guy, and he's crazy for you."

I tilted my head. "You think?"

She snorted. "I know. The way he looked at you… I mean, come on, Nova. He just fought a supernatural sociopath for you. What more does a guy need to do to prove he's into you?"

"True." I laughed. "He did risk his immortal life."

Minutes later, I pulled up to her townhouse. After she climbed out of the car, she glanced back in. "You should give this thing with Diego a chance."

"I plan to." Stealing a glance back at the vampire, who had parked behind us, I smiled.

"Good luck." Gianna beamed like a proud mama and then closed the car door.

I drove back to the house with Diego following. Despite what I'd said, it was comforting to have him there. When was the last time someone looked out for me like this?

Yes, I did want to give us a chance. Sure, we had all sorts of obstacles to deal with since only one of us was immortal, but after what we'd faced tonight, what did we have to lose?

DIEGO

Once I parked behind Nova, I rushed over to her. The torment of seeing her threatened earlier haunted me, and all I wanted to do was ensure she was safe.

I slung my arm around her waist. "How about we go inside and decompress with some Monty Python?"

She turned and glanced up at me. "That sounds like a great idea. But I have a better suggestion of what we can do first." She leaned onto her tiptoes and kissed me.

I cupped her face and responded with more intensity. After almost losing her tonight, I couldn't think of anything I wanted more than being alone with her to show her what she meant to me.

After we broke apart, I said, "One question, your bed or mine?"

She tipped her head and gave me a coquettish smile. "Both?"

Even with my speed, I couldn't move quickly enough. We entered my side of the house, and Shadow was all over us, meowing and rubbing against our legs as if he'd sensed something was wrong tonight. Once we gave him enough chin rubs to satisfy his short need for human contact, he sauntered away.

We started in her room in case the guys were home, and we were loud, but once we were naked, ended up staying there. I kissed her everywhere, overcome with almost losing her earlier, and desperate to feel her body burn with life.

After we made up with hot, sweaty, we-almost-died-tonight sex, we lay panting side-by-side. I ran my hand over the curves of her body.

"I'm so grateful to you for what you did tonight, Diego." Her eyes glistened. "I don't want to imagine what would have happened if you hadn't." Her bottom lip trembled.

I stroked her cheek as if I could brush her fears away. "Don't think about it because it didn't happen." I gulped before I admitted, "I'm here for you, Nova. Even after you go back to New York, you can call me whenever you need someone."

It felt so good to care for another person again. Maybe it was corny, but I'd been so caught up in self-hatred and despair that this new mind shift gave me a fresh lifeline.

"I've been thinking about that." Her lips tightened. "Leaving."

My gut fell to the floorboards. Why did I ruin the moment by bringing up her departure?

"What I mean is that I've been thinking more about returning to New York and realized I don't want to." She gestured with an open palm. "I've been able to do my job here, so there's no reason they shouldn't let me continue doing so. And if they don't, I'll find another job."

"They'd be foolish to let you go." I stroked her soft cheek. "I'm not crazy enough to do that."

"Good, because I have no intention of leaving. Everything I need is here. Everyone I want to be near is here." She gazed at me with warmth. "Especially you."

My eyes widened. To make sure I wasn't imagining things, I had to confirm it. "You want to stay here in Salem?"

"I do." Her lips twitched into a smile. "Hope you don't mind me moving into the house for good."

We stared into each other's eyes, and I traced my fingers over her soft cheek. All the fears I'd had about losing her vanished. Sure we had plenty of other obstacles to face to make a relationship work, but we made it through the most difficult one—taking this step to be together.

"It sounds like you even have a job offer at the Network," I said.

She laughed. "I still can't believe that. I mean, we're talking about me, someone who thought she had zero talent as a witch until recently."

"You're incredible, Nova. With magic or not. I think you're amazing." I sat up. "Hold on, I have something for you. I'll be right back."

NOVA

While Diego went to get something from his room, I relaxed on the bed to recover. Hot, sweaty, makeup sex had left me breathless. With moves like that, I'd be shouting more, more, more in no time.

When he returned a few minutes later, he held something behind his back. "I already have a small housewarming present for you."

I sat up. "How did you know I'd be staying?"

"I didn't, but I hoped." With a small grin, he added, "Actually, I bought it to let you know I was thinking about you, but then feared you might think it was weird."

"Weird? I'm intrigued." I rubbed my hands together. "What is it?"

He tossed something small, white, and fuzzy in my direction and called, "Watch out."

I caught it and squinted at the stuffed animal. What the hell was it—a bunny with fangs? Dripping with blood?

Ah, I nodded, catching on. "A killer rabbit." I chuckled. "That's hysterical. I love it." Raising my hand, I declared, "Be afraid!" I tossed it back at him.

Diego caught the stuffed toy mid-air as he leaped onto the bed. Then he wrestled with the stuffed animal as if being attacked. He held it overhead and shouted before bringing the rabbit down onto his neck.

I joined in on the fake skirmish, but couldn't stop laughing as we rolled onto the bed.

Diego ended on top of me, staring down. The laughter faded from his eyes as desire took over. Heat pooled inside me. I pulled him down onto me, and we kissed.

After Diego pulled away, he stared into my eyes. "I've fallen for you, Nova. I fall a little deeper every day."

"Oh, Diego." I pressed my hand onto my cheek. "I feel the same way. So what do you say? We give us a go?"

"Abso-freaking-lutely." He kissed me again, and we rolled across the bed.

The killer rabbit fell to the ground.

EPILOGUE

SEBASTIAN

Nova convinced us to visit her friend Gianna's club, Danger Zone, to celebrate our next chapter as housemates. Nova and Diego had gone to New York for the weekend. When they returned, they officially moved her into the house.

Lucas and I followed them into the club. Who would have thought these two would get together? Certainly not me when they'd first met. Not after Diego had been almost out of control with a thirst for her blood.

I smirked at how he'd wrapped his arm protectively around her waist. He must have been hungry for something else as well.

We entered the club, a dark room with red and purple lights shining overhead. Billy Idol's "Rebel Yell" played, and many of the women pumped their arms as they chanted along with, "More, more, more."

I nudged Lucas. "A good sign for us getting lucky tonight."

He nodded and arched his brows. "Indeed." Pointing to the bar, he said, "Let's get a drink first."

Once we sat at the bar and ordered drinks, I caught it—the scent that had been driving me crazy in recent weeks. "I smell it. Right here in this club."

It wasn't a bad smell, quite the opposite. It was alluring.

I'd scented it on Nova—sometimes.

I'd scented it in our kitchen.

And now, I scented it here, more pronounced than ever.

"Enough with that already." Diego rolled his eyes. "You keep talking about this 'scent.' It must all be in your head."

"No." I shook my head. "It started after Nova came into town." I glanced at her.

She tilted her head and teased. "Sorry, Sebastian. Not sure what it means, but I'm taken."

"That's not it. It's not you," I replied. Then what exactly was it?

It was stronger here than in the past. So feminine and enchanting. Whoever this woman was, she'd been in this spot recently. I scanned the women dancing, moving their bodies with wild abandon as they jumped around to the song.

Unable to sit still, I downed my shot of whiskey and climbed off the stool. Would I finally unravel the identify of this mysterious woman?

"Where are you going?" Lucas asked.

"To find her," I declared. "Whoever she is, wherever she is, I'm tracking her down tonight."

Author's note: Have you figured out who has been driving Sebastian crazy from afar? Read on to find out what happens next in Hot in Witch City, book 2 in Salem Supernaturals!

Thanks for reading!

Lisa

P.S. Be sure to subscribe at lisacarlislebooks.com to get your free gifts from me.

GO BEHIND THE SCENES

Want more from the stories? Want to be the first to read new books before they're released?

Join me at Patreon to go behind the scenes with music, videos, free books, and exclusive content!

https://www.patreon.com/lisacarlisle

BE A VIP READER!

ACKNOWLEDGMENTS

Here's a shout out to the team! It takes a lot of time and effort to move from the strange, random ideas to my head to a complete story. Thank you to all the people who are part of this publishing journey, including my critique group, editors, cover artists, beta readers, ARC readers, and Street Team!

And thank you to my family for their support and patience while I'm in another world, working on my stories.

Lisa

ABOUT THE AUTHOR

USA Today bestselling author Lisa Carlisle loves to write stories about wounded or misunderstood heroes finding their happily ever after. They often face the temptation of fated and forbidden love--so difficult to resist!

Her romances have been named Top Picks at Night Owl Reviews and the Romance Reviews.

She draws on her travels and experiences in her stories, which include moving to Okinawa, Japan, while in the Marines, back-packing alone through Europe, and working in Paris as an au pair before returning to the U.S. She owned a bookstore for a few years as she loves to read. She's now married to a fantastic man, and they have two kids, two cats, and too many fish.

Visit her website for more on books, trailers, playlists, and more:

Lisacarlislebooks.com

Sign up for her newsletter to hear about new releases, specials, and freebies:

http://www.lisacarlislebooks.com/subscribe/

Join her **Facebook reader group!**

Lisa loves to connect with readers. You can find her on:

Facebook

Twitter

Pinterest

Instagram

Goodreads

BOOK LIST

Salem Supernaturals

Paranormal chick lit with comedy, romance, and mystery!

- *Rebel Spell*
- *Hot in Witch City*
- *Dancing with My Elf*

Salem Supernaturals is a spin-off from the White Mountain Shifters series.

White Mountain Shifters

Escape to the magic of the White Mountains with fated mates and forbidden love in these steamy paranormal romances!

- *The Reluctant Wolf and His Fated Mate*
- *The Wolf and His Forbidden Witch*
- *The Alpha and His Enemy Wolf*

White Mountain Shifters is a spin-off from the Underground Encounters series.

Underground Encounters

Steamy paranormal romances set in an underground goth club that attracts vampires, witches, shifters, and gargoyles.

- *Book 1: SMOLDER (a vampire / firefighter romance)*
- *Book 2: FIRE (a witch / firefighter romance)*
- *Book 3: IGNITE (a feline shifter / rock star romance)*
- *Book 4: BURN (a vampire / shapeshifter rock romance)*
- *Book 5: HEAT (a gargoyle shifter romance)*

- *Book 6: BLAZE (a gargoyle shifter rockstar romance)*
- *Book 7: COMBUST (vampire / witch romances)*
- *Book 8: INFLAME (a gargoyle shifter / witch romance)*
- *Book 9: TORCH (a gargoyle shifter / werewolf romance*
- *Book 10: SCORCH (an incubus vs succubus demon romance)*

Chateau Seductions

An art colony on a remote New England island lures creative types—and supernatural characters. Steamy paranormal romances.

- *Darkness Rising*
- *Dark Velvet*
- *Dark Muse*
- *Dark Stranger*
- *Dark Pursuit*

Highland Gargoyles

Gargoyle shifters, wolf shifters, and tree witches have divided the Isle of Stone after a great battle 25 years ago. One risk changes it all…

- *Knights of Stone: Mason*
- *Knights of Stone: Lachlan*
- *Knights of Stone: Bryce*
- *Seth: a wolf shifter romance in the series*
- *Knights of Stone: Calum*
- *Stone Cursed*
- *Knights of Stone: Gavin*

Stone Sentries

Meet your perfect match the night of the super moon — or your perfect match for the night. A cop teams up with a gargoyle shifter when demons attack Boston.

- *Tempted by the Gargoyle*
- *Enticed by the Gargoyle*
- *Captivated by the Gargoyle*

Anchor Me

Navy SEALs, Marines, and hometown heroes. Each one encounters his most complicated mission yet, when he will find a woman from his past—who changes his future.

- *Antonio (a novella available for free to subscribers)*
- *Angelo*
- *Vince*
- *Matty*
- *Jack*
- *Slade*
- *Mark*

Night Eagle Operations

A paranormal romantic suspense novel

- *When Darkness Whispers*

Berkano Vampires

A shared author world with dystopian paranormal romances.

- *Immortal Resistance*

Blood Courtesans

A shared author world with the vampire blood courtesans.

- *Pursued: Mia*

Visit LisaCarlisleBooks.com to learn more!

Printed in Great Britain
by Amazon

17341759R00137